Hellraiser!

After his last indiscretion, Bass sends Josh Ford to Texas. Let him be someone else's headache for a while. The marshal there is an old friend and welcomes the badge-toting hellraiser with open arms and a whole wagonload of trouble.

Then word comes that Bass is missing and Ford swears he'll walk through the fires of Hell itself to find out what has happened to his father.

In the end, he does just that. Shoulder to shoulder with a marshal called Willis and a fast gun named Laramie Davis.

Hellraiser!

Sam Clancy

A Black Horse Western

ROBERT HALE

© Sam Clancy 2019
First published in Great Britain 2019

ISBN 978-0-7198-2916-1

The Crowood Press
The Stable Block
Crowood Lane
Ramsbury
Marlborough
Wiltshire SN8 2HR

www.bhwesterns.com

Robert Hale is an imprint
of The Crowood Press

Typeset by
Derek Doyle & Associates, Shaw Heath
Printed and bound in Great Britain by
4Bind Ltd, Stevenage, SG1 2XT

*This one is for Sam and Jacob,
and the old feller,
Michael Hickmotte Towns*

PROLOGUE

'Howdy, Mr Kemp,' the storekeeper said to a tall, grey-haired man in a black suit. 'Sure is a nice morning, ain't it?'

Oliver Kemp stopped and smiled at the man speaking to him, standing there with the straw broom he was using to sweep down the boardwalk out front of his dry goods store. 'Why yes, it is, Mr Green. Yes, it is.'

Beside Kemp stood another man, one who was younger, broader, and had a dark beard. Lacey Harper was Kemp's hired help, though technically, gunman was a more accurate job description for him. Being a wealthy man, Kemp believed that he needed one.

'Not long until the mayoral elections, Mr Kemp. Are you still going to run against Tobias?'

The smile never left Kemp's face. 'Indeed, indeed.'

'That'll be good. You'll get my vote, for sure.'

'Why, thank you, Mr Green,' Kemp said, before

reaching into his pocket and retrieving a shiny, silver pocket-watch. He opened it, studied the time and said, 'Well, Mr Green, I must be off. Breakfast awaits.'

'Sure, Mr Kemp. I'll be seeing you later?'

'For our chess game?'

'Yes.'

'I wouldn't miss it for the world. I'll see you at half-two.'

'I'll see you then. I look forward to it.'

The two men kept on. They walked past the bank, the jail, the telegraph office, saddlery, and two saloons until they reached the edge of town where the main street branched. One angled off to the right, which would take whoever travelled it, to the next town. The other continued straight up a hill towards a large, two-storey, white mansion: Kemp's home.

Showing no sign of exertion, they walked up the steep rise and through an archway of flowering wisteria in the centre of the white picket fence, along a path, up a sturdy set of steps, and across a broad veranda to a large oak door.

After entering the foyer, they removed their hats and hung them on a stand beside a wide staircase that curved grandly to the second floor. It resembled a New York hotel more than a home.

From a door to their right, a thin-faced man in a black suit emerged. He stopped in front of Kemp and said, 'Welcome home, sir. Can I get you anything?'

Kemp shook his head and gave his coat to the

man. 'No, thank you, Tennison. How is our visitor? I hope you've looked after him this morning.'

Tennison's face dropped. 'I'm afraid he's been quite uncooperative this morning, sir.'

'Hmm, I'll go and have a word with him. See if I can change his mood. That will be all, Tennison.'

'Yes, sir.'

After the butler had disappeared, Kemp turned to Harper. 'Let's go and see what the problem is this time.'

They crossed the foyer and stopped at a solid timber door. Harper opened it and Kemp entered, making his way down the stairs into a dark cavern, dimly lit by a single lamp. When the house on the hill was built, the subterranean room had been excavated, then lined with rock. It gave off a cold, unwelcome feeling.

They stopped at the foot of the stairs and stared across the gloomy room. 'What seems to be the problem today? The rats eating your food?'

A chained man snarled. 'Let me loose, you damned son of a bitch and I'll damned well eat you.'

'Oh, dear, we have woken up in a bad mood this morning.'

The man's greying hair was messy and unkempt, his face showing weeks of growth the same colour as the mustache. His clothes were filthy, and he stank of unwashed body, the smell surpassed only by the rank stench of the bucket of excrement in the corner.

The man lurched forward, dragging the thick chain with him until it snapped taut. 'Damn you to

9

hell, Kemp. You know what I'm looking at? Huh, do you?'

Kemp sighed. 'Do tell.'

'A dead man. You hear me? A dead man. When my son finds out, he'll hunt me down and fill you with so much lead it'll take ten men to carry your pine box!'

Kemp smiled. 'Oh, I hope so, Marshal. I truly hope so. You see, Josh Ford will be an integral part of my plan.'

PART 1

KILL ONE DENT, KILL THEM ALL!

CHAPTER 1

Ford hated Texas. Not the state itself, that was OK. But the fact that it was overrun with so many outlaws from both sides of the border. Desperados who killed for money or just for the hell of it.

Since being banished to the Lone Star State for his last indiscretion in a small town known as Hell, Ford had locked up or killed no fewer than seven wanted felons. And that was just in the space of three weeks. His temporary boss at the time didn't mind, though. United States Marshal Walton Grimes thought Ford was the best thing that had happened to Texas since joining the Union.

The black-clad deputy now rode into the small town of Crofton, on the trail of Manuel Ortega. It was rumoured that the Mexican fast-gun was here after he'd killed a wealthy rancher further east near San Antonio two months earlier.

United States Deputy Marshal Josh Ford usually stomped around Montana, Colorado or Wyoming bringing lawbreakers to book. Up there he was well known as a hard, do-what-it-takes peace officer. Down here in Texas they quickly learned how he operated.

He stood a touch over six feet tall and was solidly built. He had dark hair, and a week's growth of stubble adorned his face.

The mean-tempered blue roan that Ford rode sent up small puffs of fine Texas dust with every step as it walked along the main street. Even the deputy's clothes were covered in the stuff. At his right thigh was a Colt Peacemaker .45. In the saddle scabbard was a Winchester .45-.70, another weapon he was quite proficient with.

The street was busy with the afternoon rush of townsfolk going about their last-minute business. The hot Texas sun lost some of its heat as it sank lower in the western sky, shadows lengthening as it went.

The roan snorted, and Ford said in a quiet voice, 'I see him.'

To their right, out the front of a false-fronted building with the word 'Bo's' emblazoned on it, was a scruffy man dressed in worn range clothes, twin six-guns in a double gun-rig, and high leather boots.

Ford racked his brain until he recalled a name. Henry Bolton. 'The Bolt', or 'Lightning Bolt' as he liked to call himself. He was a tenth-rate hired gun out of Colorado, with paper on his head. The deputy made a mental note to look up Bolton after he'd dealt with Ortega.

The roan continued past a small mercantile, a saddlery, a lands office, and a dozen other businesses that lined the street. Ford also noted the three large, false-fronted saloons. One was named the Prairie Rose, another the Desert Springs, and the third was called simply Gutshot.

A grim smile came to Ford's face: 'Nice!'

It was not until Ford had ridden another twenty yards along the street that he understood why Grimes had sent him. The town was a nest of rattlers. For in that twenty yards he saw another three outlaws and two more gunmen.

Ford shook his head as he realized that his task seemed almost insurmountable, and considered what it entailed. 'That cunning old goat knew what he was doing. Now a feller knows why he was smiling like a cat who ate the chicken when I rode out.'

A hot wind blew along the street, kicking up dust as it went. The roan snorted again, this time in protest as the grit hit its face.

Ford nodded. 'Yeah, tell me about it. I've got more dust inside my shirt than I have on the outside.'

A little further along the street, Ford found the jail. It was a small, false-fronted affair with plank walls and a large front window, which enabled the local sheriff to see outside from his desk. With the roan tied at the hitch rail, Ford stomped up the steps and swatted dust from his clothes. He crossed the uneven plank boardwalk and entered the office through a timber door.

Ford found the local sheriff at his desk with his feet up on its scarred surface. Unsure at first, his instincts told him that the man was asleep.

14

He was right. The man snorted and then squirmed to make himself more comfortable in his chair. Ford raised his Winchester and brought the butt down firmly on the desktop. The noise startled the slumbering man and brought him lurching to his feet.

'Glory be. What on earth?'

'Are you what passes for law in this town?'

The sheriff blinked to clear his blurred vision. 'Who the hell are you?'

'The name's Ford, Deputy United States Marshal. Who are you?'

'Fletcher. Sheriff Ike Fletcher.'

'Not one for doing your job, are you?'

Fletcher frowned. 'Huh?'

'When I rode into Crofton, I saw four wanted men and two hired guns. Add to that the supposed fact that Manuel Ortega is in town. So tell me, what is it you actually *do* around here?'

Fletcher just stared at him.

Ford's voice hardened. 'Let me ask you this. Why are you still sheriff if you can't do your job?'

Again there was only a stunned silence.

Finally, Ford ran out of patience. 'Take off the badge.'

'Huh?'

'I said, take off the blasted badge. Are you hard of hearing?'

'Why?'

' 'Cause you just retired.'

'Mr Bartlett. . . .' Fletcher stopped and then said, 'You can't do this. You got no right.'

Ford pointed the Winchester at the centre of Fletcher's face and thumbed back the hammer. 'This gives me all the right I need. Now take off the God-damned badge.'

Fletcher hesitated a moment before removing the badge, and threw it on to the desk top with a clunk. He then gave Ford a cold look. 'Mr Bartlett won't like this.'

Ford shot him a cold smile. 'You tell Mr Bartlett that if he has a problem, to come and see me. Now, get out of my sight.'

Ford watched him go, and then looked around the jail. On the far wall he saw a gun-rack with a cut-down shotgun and two Winchesters. On a peg near a door that led out the back were the keys to the cells.

It wasn't long before Ford had a visit from the man named Bartlett. He was a round man in a suit and a put-upon disposition. When he entered the jail he looked Ford up and down and snapped, 'Who do you think you are, coming in and taking over?'

Ford sighed. 'I take it that you're Bartlett?'

Bartlett nodded. 'I am. And this is my town. There is law here already. We don't need you.'

Ford was about to speak when another man entered the jail. He wore dark pants with silver trims, a red shirt and a large sombrero. His face was a walnut-brown colour and sported a large black moustache. It had to be Manuel Ortega.

'I wasn't sent here to be no local law. I came here with a job to do. It just so happens that when I arrived I saw how lacking law actually was.'

'Then you do your job and ride on.'

16

'I aim to do just that. After I do what needs to be done.'

Bartlett nodded. 'Good. I believe we understand each other.'

Ford ran his gaze over Ortega. The gunfighter had a presence about him, sure, but it wasn't anything the deputy marshal hadn't seen before. The Mexican noticed and smiled coldly at him.

'We'll be going then.'

'You can. But your man, Ortega there, ain't going anywhere.'

The gunfighter was suddenly poised. 'What you say, gringo?'

'I said you ain't going nowhere. Are you deaf?'

Bartlett moved to calm the situation. 'Whoa, Marshal. I don't think you realize what you're doing.'

'I know exactly what I'm doing. I'm arresting a cold-blooded killer.'

Ortega's hand formed a claw above his gun butt. 'You really want to go down this path, gringo lawman?'

Ford's gaze turned to stone. 'I tell you what, Mex, I'll give you to the count of three to get rid of that fancy gun-rig around your waist. If you fail to do so, then I'll shoot you where you stand.'

Ortega smiled again and looked at Bartlett.

'Don't look at him. I'm the feller who's going to kill you.'

The Mexican's eyes grew devoid of emotion as he stared back at Ford. The corner of his mouth flickered up and then he snarled as he went for his gun,

'You are the one who will die!'

Ford's Peacemaker came free of his holster in one fluid motion. The hammer was back and ready to fire by the time it was level. He squeezed the trigger and the Colt bucked in his fist. The slug punched into Ortega's chest, slamming his body against the wall behind him. His six-gun hadn't even cleared leather.

The Peacemaker swivelled to cover Bartlett, who stood there, stunned. 'Did you say you were leaving?'

Bartlett turned his troubled gaze towards the deputy and nodded jerkily. 'You haven't heard the last of this.'

'Don't push me, Bartlett. You won't win.'

After the shaken man left, Ford looked down at the dead Mexican. Well, that was one down. But there were more. And before he was finished, there was bound to be trouble.

A noise in the doorway made him raise the unholstered Peacemaker. Flinching reflexively, a black-clad man with a tall top hat stepped back and put his hands up.

Ford placed the six-gun back in his holster: 'Sorry.'

The expression on the man's wrinkled face eased. 'My name is Jubal. I'm the undertaker.'

Ford nodded. 'Ford, United States Deputy Marshal.'

Jubal indicated the body on the floor. 'Could you give me a hand to carry him to my place of work?'

But Ford had turned away and was taking down a sawn-off shotgun from the rack on the wall. He checked to see that it was loaded before walking back across to the desk, where he found some spare shells. When he turned around, he looked at the undertaker and said, 'Sorry, I'm going to be busy.'

Ford cursed as he looked along the deserted main street. OK, almost deserted. Beneath his shirt sleeve he could feel blood flowing down his left arm to his fingertips; from there it dripped into the thirsty grey dust at his feet.

In his right hand was the Peacemaker, a thin line of gun smoke rising from its barrel. By his estimation, there should still be two more rounds in it. More than he needed to kill Henry Bolton.

A moan drew his attention. Twenty feet in front of him, hunched over on his knees, was Bartlett. Ford had shot the fat man through his ample gut when he'd produced a hideout gun and tried to shoot him.

Further along the street was one of the outlaws he'd seen when he arrived. The man lay dead next to a horse trough, his chest a mess of bloody rags from the charge of buckshot.

Another was bent double over a hitch rail, his six-gun at his feet where it had fallen. The third was dead in the mouth of an alleyway where he'd tried to bushwhack Ford.

The gunmen, except for Bolton, were different. They'd come after him hard and fast. None of that bushwhack horseshit, just a straight-up, good old-fashioned frontal assault. Not that it had done them any good.

They'd died within ten feet of one another, .45

caliber slugs buried in their chests.

That left Bolton. He was the one who'd shot Ford. The dirty yellow skunk came out of the Gutshot Saloon behind Ford and tried to ambush him. Which was how the deputy found himself bleeding and angry. Then the gunman had disappeared back into the saloon.

Ford shook his head. 'Bolton! Get the hell out here, you coward!'

A high-pitched voice filtered outside. 'Why don't you come and get me, Marshal?'

Ford's arm throbbed. Minute by minute his anger grew faster than a rattlesnake with its tail stomped on.

'If I come in there after you, there is no way you'll be alive once it's all over!'

The answer was a gunshot that hissed close to Ford's ear, which only served to irritate the deputy even more.

The hammer of the Peacemaker was thumbed back as it dangled near Ford's thigh. He set his jaw firm and strode towards the Gutshot Saloon with a deadly purpose in each step.

Fletcher emerged from an alley to Ford's right, a cocked six-gun in his hand. The weapon roared, and splinters were chewed from an awning upright behind Ford. The deputy fired once, and with a cry of pain, the once sheriff of Crofton threw his arms in the air and went down.

One bullet left.

When Ford pushed in through the batwings, the

interior of the saloon erupted with gunfire. Those within earshot might have thought a full-blown battle had broken out in the two-storey establishment. But once the abrupt flurry of shots ceased, a single gunshot sounded.

Only then did a heavy silence descend upon the town, an eeriness punctuated by the clunk of boots on floorboards. They stopped momentarily, before the squeak of dry hinges indicated the opening of the batwings once more.

Ford stepped out on to the boardwalk and halted. Blood still dripped from his fingertips, this time forming a small pool on the scarred and dusty planks. In his right hand was the empty Peacemaker.

Ford looked up and down the street. He could see townsfolk emerging tentatively from their various places of refuge. He sucked in a deep breath and let it out slowly. Then he said out loud, 'Damn, I hate Texas.'

CHAPTER 2

When Ford rode into the town of Three Forks, Texas, United States Marshal Walton Grimes was sitting in a wicker chair out front of his office, enjoying the morning sun.

Grimes was a solidly built man in his forties with dark hair and moustache. With intense outlaw activity in Three Forks for some time, he'd been transferred there about a year before to sort things out. He'd requested more marshals to help out, but those pleas had fallen on deaf ears. Then word had come from his old friend Bass Reeves, that his son was on the way and to use him as he saw fit.

Ford's reputation had preceded him through various channels and the marshal was pleased for the help. When the bodies started to pile up, he began to think that Ford could be really useful.

Word had been filtering out of Crofton for a while now about Bartlett and his influence over the town. And when Grimes had heard about Ortega showing up there, well, the opportunity was too good to pass up.

He'd sent Ford.

Now the marshal from up north was riding up the main street, a string of nine pack-horses in tow, attracting all manner of attention from the townsfolk as every horse was carrying a ripe corpse draped over its back.

The stench of death reached Grimes well before Ford did. The marshal screwed up his nose at the assault on his sense, and climbed from his chair. Once erect he walked out into the street.

When Ford drew level on the blue roan, Grimes' face pinched in disgust. 'What in tarnation are you doing trailing all that?'

'All *that* as you refer to it, is what you sent me to Crofton for. Sure, you sent me there to get Ortega. But you knew what else I would find there, didn't you? Well, here they are.'

He dropped the lead rope to the ground and turned the roan away.

'Hey, where are you going?'

'For a bath,' Ford called back.

'What about these? You can't leave them there.'

'Yeah, I can.'

Grimes looked at the body-laden horses, and in spite of the stench, gave a mirthless smile. Ford may not be there for long, but he sure would make the most out of the situation. And for that reason, he already had a notion of where to send Ford next.

A little town called Dent.

*

The Cow Hide Saloon was busy that afternoon when Grimes found Ford. Cowmen were bellied up to a long bar as they talked about their week, while here and there a soiled dove was draped over one of them, helping to part them from their hard-earned cash. Cigar smoke built up steadily with each passing hour, and before the night was out, would hang thickly in the air like an early morning fog. Behind the bar, a squinty-eyed keep known as Bill was kept busy moving back and forth filling empty glasses and providing fresh bottles.

Both marshals sat in a far corner, out of the way but still able to keep an eye on things. Not that town stuff was their problem. Three Forks had a sheriff for that. But old habits die hard.

Ford put the half-empty glass down on the scarred tabletop and looked curiously at Grimes. He cocked an eyebrow and asked, 'What did you say the name of this town was?'

'Dent.'

'And the name of this feller is. . . ?'

'Hiram Dent.'

'That's what I thought you said. This ain't going to be a job like the last one you sent me on, is it?'

'Weeell . . .'

Ford rolled his eyes. 'Uh huh. Who is he? Is the town named after him or something?'

'No, not after him,' Grimes said truthfully.

Ford picked up the whiskey glass. 'That's something.'

24

'It was named after his pappy.'

The empty glass smacked down on the tabletop again. 'Son of a bitch, Grimes. Are you set on killing me or something? I bet the damn town is full of Dents. The *hombre* has probably got ten brothers waiting to shoot anyone who comes after him.'

'Oh, no. No, not at all. That's an exaggeration if I ever heard one. He only has six.'

Sarcasm dripped from Ford's voice. 'That's just wonderful. I can see the headstone now. *Here lies Josh Ford. Shot full of holes by Dents.*'

'Have you finished?'

Ford growled as he picked up the two-thirds full bottle of whiskey and poured another drink. 'I'm only just getting started.'

'Listen, Josh. Hiram Dent shot a sheriff over in the town of Hadley. He needs to be brought in. His pappy is the orneriest son of a bitch I ever knew. He'd do anything for that boy of his. Including shoot any lawman who came after him.'

'Well, why haven't *you* brought him in yet then?'

'I sent two marshals after him in the past two months. The last one was sent back to me wrapped up in barbed wire and tied to his horse. Your pa said you were good at what you do. And going by what you did over in Crofton, I'd have to agree with him. Yes, the job is dangerous. Your pa said you were the best. That's what I need.'

'And what if all these Dents try to stop me? I want to be clear on how far you want me to go to bring him in. A job like this, I can't have my hands tied.'

Grimes' face became a harsh mask. 'You do what-ever it takes. Even if you have to kill them all to do it. I'm beyond caring.'

'Where do you want me to take him? Assuming I take him alive, that is.'

'Take him to Hadley. He'll be tried there. The new sheriff's name is Pete Newey. I've met him, seems like a decent feller.'

'What do you want me to do after I drop him off there?'

'Hang around for a few days and make sure there's no trouble. I'm not saying there will be, but them Dents are a breed of their own. Like as not they'll follow you there and try to break him out. And don't go into the swamp.'

That got Ford's attention. 'What swamp? Where is this Dent anyway?'

'Harrison County.'

Ford shook his head in bemusement. 'You mean Texas, Louisiana, border swamp?'

'Yeah.'

'Let me guess. Snakes, gators, big hairy swamp men?'

'Brewsters.'

'What?'

'They're called Brewsters, and trust me, you don't want to go into their swamp.'

Ford nodded. 'Anything else?'

Grimes reached across the table to grab the bottle so he could refill his glass. 'Nope. I think that's enough. Don't you?'

Ford grimaced as the wound on his arm gave a twinge, and he thought about the myriad of unfortunate possibilities that could occur with the whole situation.

A grim smile touched Ford's lips. 'Nope. I'd say that was more than enough.'

'Cheer up, you'll be fine.'

A flattened hunk of lead chewed splinters from the corner of the building where Ford was sheltered and whined harmlessly past the deputy marshal as he jacked another round into the Winchester's breech.

'I sure wish people would damned well stop telling me I'll be fine, all the time,' he growled in a low voice.

'You don't really think you're going to get out of town do you, Marshal?' the voice of young Hiram Dent cackled from behind him. 'Not alive, anyways.'

Ford snapped and fired a shot across the street at a crouched form scurrying towards some water barrels. 'Shut up, Hiram.'

The man screamed and stumbled forwards on to his face. He lay there unmoving, and Ford could only assume he was dead.

Hiram Dent flared. 'You son of a bitch. That was my cousin, Joey.'

A snarl of rage escaped Ford's lips as he snapped off another shot. 'I wish someone had told me about your cousins before I came here. Damn it!'

Ford had arrived shortly after noon, badge in his pocket. There was no point riding into the lion's den advertising the fact that he was a lawman.

After a few discreet enquiries, he'd ascertained who Hiram Dent was and proceeded to arrest him.

Ford thought he'd planned it well. Find Hiram Dent, put him on a horse that Ford supplied, and ride out of town before things heated up too much. That was before he'd found out about the cousins, uncles, aunts, and every other damned Dent in the black hole of a town.

He could only assume that it was one of them who'd shot the horse he'd brought along for Hiram, which lay in the middle of the street, along with another Dent. Anyhow, it was too late to worry about that. Somehow he had to get Hiram out of town without getting himself killed.

Ford looked at the bodies in the street. With Joey now out of action, the tally had risen to four. Which, by his calculations, still left far too many Dents and their kin to deal with.

That was not counting the old man and his hired ranch hands. Ford guessed he wouldn't be far away. Then he could most likely count on a swift but violent death. Something to look forward to.

Somehow Ford needed to gain the upper hand long enough to get the kid out of town and away from his kin.

Too late. The thunder of hoofbeats could be heard above the gunfire and this concerned Ford no end. For the sound to be heard meant. . . .

The riders swung into view around the dogleg in the main street. At their head rode a grey-haired man on a white horse.

'Great. Your old man knows how to make an entrance, Hiram.'

'Are you pissing in your boots already, Marshal?'

Ford figured the patriarch to have somewhere in the region of twenty men with him. Too many for him to shoot it out with.

Quickly, he glanced about for somewhere suitable to hole up. Then he spotted it. A false-fronted shop across the street with a big yellow sign above the awning which read: DENT SUPPLIES.

Ford turned around and walked across to where Hiram was seated, hands tied behind his back. He leaned down and grabbed him by the collar.

Ford dragged him erect. 'Get up.'

His actions brought forth a string of curses. 'What the hell are you doing, lawdog?'

'Just shut up and do what I tell you. Come on, horse.'

Then, with the barrel of the Winchester pressed firmly against the back of Hiram's head, they walked out into the open, the blue roan close behind.

As they stopped in the middle of the rutted main street, Ford heard voices shout, 'Hold your fire!'

The riders hauled back on their horses' reins and brought them to a noisy halt. Ford saw the deep lines in old man Dent's features, just before a large cloud of dust kicked up by the horses engulfed him and Hiram.

The dust cloud was so thick that to the naked eye it was impenetrable.

'What the hell?' one of the riders cursed out loud.

Through it all, the gravelly voice of Charlie Dent could be heard. 'Spread out. Get ready for when this dust settles. And for chrissakes, watch where you're shooting. If any one of you hits my boy, I'll skin him alive.'

'I can't see nothing, boss,' one cowhand complained.

'Me neither,' another said.

'Just wait, damn it,' Dent growled. 'It'll clear directly.'

Clear it did, and before them was an empty street.

'Christ, where the hell did they go, boss?'

CHAPTER 3

Hiram yelped loudly, his cry filling the dim interior of the supplies store. 'Son of a bitch! He bit me!'

'If you don't shut up I'll let him bite you again.'

The mean-tempered blue roan snorted. The horse was far from happy about being cooped up in such a confined space.

Ford looked at the man who ran the store. 'We'll be out of here soon.'

From where he stood at his serving desk, the man nodded. Ford turned to look out the window and by the time he looked back, the store owner had emerged from behind the counter with a sawn-off shotgun in his hand.

A cheerful shout from Hiram filled the room. 'That's it, cousin Jeb. Shoot the son of a bitch.'

The Peacemaker in Ford's hand came up and roared to life. The .45 caliber slug punched into Jeb Dent's chest, knocking him backward, discharging the shotgun into the ceiling as he went down.

Hiram's face fell. 'You just keep killing my kin,

Marshal. But you can't kill us all.'

Ford turned back to the window. 'I can damned well try.'

Outside, the horses milled around, and then one of the riders pointed at the mining supplies store.

'Damn it,' Ford swore for the umpteenth time.

He cast a hurried glance around the store for anything he could use, then noticed the storeroom door.

The deputy marshal looked at Hiram Dent and scowled, 'You move from here and you won't see the sun go down.'

He glowered. 'I know who ain't going to see the sun go down, Marshal. And it ain't me.'

Ford ignored him and hurried across to the storeroom door. He opened it and stepped into the gloom. Spotting something he could use, the corner of his mouth lifted.

'Marshal!' the voice filtered in from out on the street.

Ford snapped his head around and looked towards the window.

'We know you're in there, Marshal. You got five minutes to let my boy go or we're coming in after you.'

The deputy marshal looked at Hiram who wore a confident smile once again.

This was going to be interesting.

'God damn it, Marshal, you can't do this! It ain't right!'

Hiram Dent bleated like a lamb as Ford put the

finishing touches to his plan. He stood back and admired his craftsmanship. He'd wrapped a rope tight around the killer's upper body and then tucked sticks of dynamite into it at random. Chances were, if someone fired a stray round, Dent would go out with a bang. A damned big one.

'Time's up, Marshal!'

Ford crossed to the window and looked out. The cowboys riding for Charlie Dent had set up barricades along the road where they had taken cover. The old man himself stood out front, his posture demanding that he be answered.

'Do you hear me, Marshal? Let my son go and we'll let you be. Just take your horse and get the hell out of Dent.'

Ford scooped up his Winchester and walked over to Hiram. He wrapped a toughened hand in the killer's collar and started to drag him towards the door.

'What are you doing?'

'Just shut up.'

Ford placed him in front of the door and then opened it. He hid out of sight to the side and then called out to Charlie Dent.

'Can you hear me, Dent?'

'I hear you.'

'Can you see your boy?'

'Just. What's that he's got tied to him?'

Ford looked at Hiram and jerked his head. 'Out the door.'

'What?'

33

Ford eared back the hammer on his rifle and pointed it at Hiram's head. 'Door. Out. Now.'

Dent took a few tentative steps through the doorway, his face beaded in nervous perspiration. 'Don't shoot, Pa! Don't shoot! The son of a bitch is crazy. Lookit he did.'

'Stop there,' said Ford.

Hiram did as ordered.

Charlie called out to his son, his voice containing a confused edge. 'Is that what I think it is, boy?'

'Yeah, Pa. It's dynamite.'

Ford stayed where he was inside. Out of sight, he wrapped a string around more dynamite to form a bundle of five sticks, figuring to use it when needed.

Charlie Dent's voice rose in pitch. 'What is this, Marshal? What do you think you're doing? You're the law. You can't do this.'

'Do you figure he'll go up like a stump?' Ford asked.

'What?'

Ford chuckled. 'He will if one of your men accidentally puts a bullet in one of them sticks.'

'That's not funny!'

Ford finished tying a knot. 'Damn, I'll have to find some new material.'

'What do you want, Marshal?'

'I want a horse for your son, and free passage out of here.'

'So you can take him away to be hanged?'

Ford stuck a fuse in the center stick of dynamite. 'The way I see it, you got two choices. You let us out

34

of here and the state hangs your son. Or you can be responsible for your son's death if the dynamite goes up.'

'Not much of a choice.'

'More of a choice than the peace officers who came before me got.'

'I had nothing to do with them,' Charlie Dent pointed out.

'Maybe not, but I bet you knew about them.'

'You know you'll never make it to where you're taking Hiram, don't you?'

Ford finished tying the last piece of string and shouted, 'You've got until sundown, Charlie. After that, we'll come out anyway. Except I'll be dragging Hiram behind my horse. I don't think the law will worry how he gets there, or even if it's in one piece.'

'He's crazy, Pa,' Hiram called almost hysterically to his father.

There was a pause in the conversation and Ford waited for something to happen. Instead, Charlie Dent shouted, 'What's your name, Marshal?'

'Ford. Josh Ford.'

'All right, Marshal Ford, you'll get your horse.'

Ford nodded with satisfaction. 'Hiram, get your murdering ass back in here.'

The rancher's son returned to the relative safety of the gloomy store. 'What now?'

Ford pointed to a barrel in the far corner. 'Take a seat and don't move.'

As he walked past the blue roan, the horse made to bite him, however, it stopped when Ford snapped,

'You do and I'll leave you here for the rest of the Dents to eat. They kinda strike me as people who'd like a good feed of horse, being inbred the way they are.'

The horse gave him an unhappy snort and let Hiram Dent be. Ford could see the horse was becoming even more cantankerous than normal and said, 'It's only until nightfall. Then we'll get the hell out of here.'

They brought a horse to the hitch rail outside the store an hour later. It was a bay, and one look told Ford that Charlie Dent had picked the sorriest looking animal the town had to offer.

Across the street, they watched and waited for Ford to make his next move.

Eventually it was Hiram who broke the silence. 'You ain't going to make it out of here, Ford.'

'You mean like those others who came before me?'

'Something like that.'

'Your pa going to tie me up in barbed wire like the last marshal he sent back? What was that, anyway? Why would you need barbed wire out in a swamp?'

Hiram nodded, a smirk on his face. 'We got to keep the cows out somehow, besides, we ain't in the swamp, just on the edge of it. Pa has cattle west of here.'

He paused and remembered the question. 'It were a goodun, weren't it? Except, Pa was telling the truth about that when he said he had nothing to do with it. That was me and brother Billy.'

Ahh yes, the other Dent brothers. 'I gather your brothers weren't in town today.'

Hiram shook his head. 'Nope, they was all doing other things. They're here now though. I seen them out there, just waiting to put a bullet in you.'

Ford leaned back in the timber chair he was sitting in, his Winchester across his lap.

'Whose idea was it to tie the marshal up in the barbed wire? Yours? Your brother's?'

A look of pride crossed Hiram's face. 'That was all mine, that one. The son of a bitch came sniffing around here looking to take me back to hang. I was in town with Billy when cousin Abel came and told me about it. The best part was, he'd gone and given the marshal a little love tap on his head and locked him up in his storeroom.'

'Cousin Abel?'

'Sure. He owns the drygoods store. He also happened to have some barbed wire there too. We killed him there, after we had a chat, of course, then we did the whole barbed wire thing. After that, we just turned his horse loose. We figured he'd go back home.'

'What about the first marshal?'

'Jake killed him. Actually, truth be known, Abel went to Jake first about the second marshal too before he came to us. Jake told him to get Billy and me to sort it out on account he was busy doing something else.'

'Jake your brother too?'

'Oldest.'

Ford's mouth set in a thin line as he fought the urge to punch Hiram in the face. Eventually he asked, 'Why the barbed wire?'

Hiram shrugged. 'Figured it'd be a good warning. I guess they didn't take any notice though, 'cause you turned up.'

There was a grim expression on Ford's face as he stored the names away in his brain for a later date. Maybe pass them on to the rangers who might send in a company to clean out this nest of vipers.

'I'm thinking that if Pa takes you alive, I might persuade him to send you back in pieces. Do you reckon Marshal Grimes will like that?'

Ford frowned. 'How do you know Grimes?'

'His son told me.'

Ford's eyebrows shot up. 'His son?'

Hiram's laugh rang loud throughout the room. 'Ha! Didn't the old buzzard tell you?'

'Tell me what?'

'About his son, of course.'

Ford grew impatient and it showed. 'Stop talking in damned riddles, Hiram.'

Hiram shook his head in bewilderment. 'I'll be. . . . He didn't tell you. The feller we tied up with barbed wire and sent back. His name was Clay Grimes. He was the old bastard's son.'

Ford's mind reeled. Why hadn't Grimes told him about it?

Hiram laughed again. 'I can't believe he sent you here and he didn't tell you. Ha ha ha.'

*

'They'll be lucky if that horse makes it two miles before it drops dead on the trail.'

Looking up at the rail-thin man standing before the battered saloon table, Charlie Dent sat with a half-empty bottle of rye in front of him. Beside it was a full glass of the tea-brown liquid.

Most of the people in the Dent Saloon were either Dents, related to Dents, or worked for them. Even the balding barkeep was a Dent.

The saloon itself was in need of repair. A wall-panel here, a chair there, a balustrade on the stairs that led up to the landing, even the brass footrail along the base of the bar. But considering all of this, overall, it was rather well presented.

Charlie nodded and said, 'Good boy, Mart. Once they're out of town, it might be easier to kill that damned marshal.'

'What about the dynamite?'

It was the question on the lips of every man gathered around the rancher. Charlie toyed with the full glass and then looked up at his son, Jake, who was the biggest of the boys and had sandy hair.

The others were there too. Billy, Cort, Gray, Joe and Mart.

'Go home and get your Sharps, Jake,' Charlie ordered. 'After they leave here, we'll trail them until morning. You can set up and take a shot once it's daylight. Shouldn't need more than one.'

'All right, Pa.'

'Why don't you just let Jake shoot Hiram, Pa,' said Gray. 'He always said he wanted to go out with a bang.'

The other brothers chuckled at the comment. Not Charlie, however. He glared at his son and growled, 'I shoulda punched your ma in the mouth the day you were born, boy. How a man could end up with such an idiot son is beyond me.'

Gray returned his father's glare. 'I guess the apple didn't fall far from the tree, hey, Pa.'

Charlie Dent lurched from his chair. 'I'll wail that sass out of you, boy, if you don't watch that mouth of yours.'

All of those who stood close to Gray, stepped away from the broad-shouldered young man; except for Cort.

'Ease up, Pa,' he said in his customary drawl.

'What did you say, boy?'

'I said, ease up.'

'Just 'cause you been away for the past two years, Cort, don't mean you can come back here and tell your pa what to do.'

Cort had been back in Dent for a week now, and as far as the Dent brothers went, he was the furthermost apple to fall from the so-called Dent tree.

In his late twenties, he wasn't tall as such, just a shade over six feet. He was, however, solidly built with powerful shoulders. His jaw was square, his hair black. About his hips he wore a gunbelt with holster tied low. In it was a Peacemaker .45 with walnut grips, polished from a lot of use.

No one knew, or cared, where he'd blown in from. He wasn't there and then he was. His father's reaction to his reappearance was a simple, *I see you're back.*

'You're digging more trouble than you can re-bury, Pa, going up against a United States Marshal.'

'Who asked you?' Charlie snapped.

A chuckle from Joe was followed by, 'A badge didn't much matter about the last two who came to Dent. Did it, Billy?'

A cold smile settled on Billy's lips. 'Nope. Not one bit.'

'You mean this has happened before?'

Billy nodded. 'Sure did. Grimes sent two of his marshals. One was his son. Me and Hiram sent him back special delivery. All trussed up in bob wire. Same as we'll do with this feller.'

'Don't go getting too excited,' Charlie growled. 'This feller seems different.'

Cort looked at his father. 'So that was what the marshal was on about before? When he said about those who came before him?'

'They came here after your brother!' Charlie snarled. 'They would have hanged him if they could have got him out of town. And no, I didn't tell Hiram and Billy to kill them. But if it had come to it, I would've done it myself.'

'Well, you got one thing right, you old fool.'

Charlie's eyes narrowed. 'What was that?'

'This marshal ain't going to be no pushover. Not Ford.'

Charlie's eyebrows lifted. 'You know him?'

Cort nodded. 'I know of him. Before I come back here, I was working up Montana and Wyoming way. His name may not be well known down here, but up there, he's damned near a legend.'

'One thing I know about legends, boy,' Charlie's voice held menace, 'is that they die. That's your brother he has over there, Cort. Don't that count for anything?'

'What did Hiram do, Pa?'

'He shot a man in Hadley. Says it was self-defence.'

Cort shot his father a sceptical look. 'If it was self-defence, Pa, why are the marshals involved?'

Charlie mumbled something under his breath that Cort couldn't quite make out.

'Speak up, Pa, I can't damned well hear you.'

Charlie's eyes flashed. 'Don't you speak to me like that, boy. I'm still your pa, and I could still whip you to a standstill.'

'Who, damn it?'

'The Hadley sheriff!' Charlie roared, his face purple with rage.

Cort rolled his eyes. 'For Chris'sakes, Pa. Let the marshal take him. It sounds to me like he's outta control. What happens if you kill another marshal? Do you know? They'll send another. Or maybe even the Texas Rangers.'

'You should know,' a new voice said.

Cort turned to face the speaker. 'You keep out of this, Hogue.'

Charlie's interest was piqued. 'Just hold on a minute. What do you mean, Hogue?'

Hogue Polsen was one of those who didn't have the last name Dent, but was a relative somewhere along the line. He looked warily at Cort before he

42

said, 'I was kind of curious as to what Cort has been doing since he was gone. After all, he didn't say.'

'No one asked,' Cort snapped.

'So when I went to Hazard a couple of days back, I picked up a paper from up north. Some city feller brought it down with him on the stage. It had a picture of Cort on the front of it. Anyhow, it seems he's been up in Kansas, working for a feller called Hooper.'

Charlie was growing impatient. 'Yeah, so?'

'Hooper was sheriff of Hays City.'

Charlie's eyes narrowed and he shifted his gaze to Cort. 'Really.'

'Seems your boy is good with a gun, Charlie,' Hogue said. 'Never knew that, did you?'

Charlie shook his head. 'Nope, I did notice he was wearing it different, though.'

Hogue continued, 'Anyway, it seems he's been back in Texas longer than we figured. A month longer, in fact.'

'Damn it, Hogue, get on with it!'

'He was in Austin before he came here. At Texas Ranger headquarters.'

Suddenly the Colt in Cort's holster leaped into his hand. 'I think this is where I leave.'

Charlie's gaze grew cold. 'You're a Texas Ranger, are you?'

'I am now. I was a deputy sheriff for a while before I came back to Texas.'

'So why are you here? You spying on your family, Cort? Gone and turned traitor, maybe?'

Cort nodded. 'With all the stories the rangers were

hearing about this place, they asked me to come and find out what was going on. Stories were right, I guess, Pa. I knew you were a tough old sonuver, but you've done lost it now. Murdering peace officers. What for? To keep Hiram from hanging for killing a sheriff? Let the marshal take him, Pa. He's no good. He's always been no good.'

'What about Billy? You want to hang him too?' Charlie snarled.

Cort nodded. 'He'll have to pay for what he did. But you need to stop this before it goes too far. You're dragging the rest of our kin in too. If you keep this up, Austin will send a whole company of rangers in here to clean the town out.'

Charlie Dent gave his son a look of contempt and spat on the floor. 'You're a traitor, boy. Plain and simple. You'd hang your own brothers.'

'There ain't much choice, Pa.'

'There's always a choice!' Charlie roared. 'If your ma could see you now.'

'I'd say she's better off where she is, wouldn't you?'

Anger flared in Charlie's eyes and, in spite of the six-gun pointed at him, the old rancher lunged at his son, hands made up into fists.

Cort met his forward movement with a solid left because his gun was in his right. It was a stinging blow that brought his father up short. The rancher rocked back on his heels, shook his head, and prepared to have another crack at Cort.

He spat blood on the floor and gave Cort a bloody-toothed grin. 'I'm going to rip your arms off and feed them to you, boy.'

'Don't do it, Pa. Don't. . . .'

Cort grunted and slumped forward to the floor. The Peacemaker fell from his grip to clatter on the floorboards. A puzzled expression crossed Charlie's face and then he saw the reason for Cort's fall.

Billy had chosen the distraction as the perfect time to come in behind his brother and club him with the six-gun in his fist. 'Son of a bitch ain't taking me back to hang.'

Charlie looked at Gray and Mart. 'Get him upstairs and locked away in a room. I'll deal with him after we're finished with this.'

The two brothers bent down and picked Cort up, dragging him away roughly. In the far corner of the barroom, a man dressed in a pinstriped suit and bowler hat slowly rose from his seat and slipped outside.

CHAPTER 4

Ford thought he was hearing things at first. He shook his head and frowned. Nope, it was still there. An urgent knocking coming from the back room of the mining supplies store.

Outside, the sun was low in the sky and in another hour or so it would be dark. Inside, the gloom was already closing in.

Ford rose from where he was seated and drew his Peacemaker. He started to cross the room and then paused. He faced Hiram and fixed him with a hard stare. 'If you've moved when I get back, I'm going to shoot you in the knee so you won't do it again.'

Without waiting for a response, Ford turned and walked into the back room.

The knocking was louder. Looking around the room, he spotted a door behind a pile of crates. He moved over to them and said, 'What do you want?'

'You have to let me in. I have something to tell you, Marshal Ford.'

'Who are you?'

'James Bowen.'

'Who?'

'James L. Bowen.'

Ford's eyebrows knitted. What on earth was he doing here? The only James L. Bowen he knew was a damned dime novelist.

He said, 'Go away.'

'I need to talk to you. Let me in.'

'Why?'

'Because they've got a plan you should know about, and they also have themselves another prisoner I think they'll kill if you don't stop them.'

While he cursed under his breath, Ford cleared the back door and opened it to reveal an average built man in a suit.

'Get in here, quick,' he ordered Bowen.

Once Bowen was inside, Ford faced and glared at him. 'What the hell are you doing in Texas? Here anyway? This ain't no place for you.'

'I . . .' Bowen stopped because Ford had turned and was walking out of the small room.

The dime novelist followed him hurriedly into the main room, and Ford halted, awaiting his answer.

Bowen looked about him. One sight of the dead man on the floor, and the roan inside, seemed to make him even more apprehensive and he blanched. Then there was Hiram Dent.

'What have you got there, Marshal? Some kind of dude by the looks of him.'

Bowen looked indignant. 'I'll have you know I'm an accomplished author, sir.'

47

Hiram pulled a face at Bowen and smirked.

Ford interrupted before he could be drawn further into the conversation with the killer. 'Tell me what you want and then be gone, Bowen.'

Bowen shot a nervous glance at Hiram and then looked back at Ford. 'They're planning to follow you out of town and ambush you. The old man sent one of his sons home for a Sharps.'

Ford nodded. 'Is that it?'

The scribbler opened his mouth to say more when a low groan from outside on the street was followed by the sound of a thud. The deputy marshal looked at Bowen and then crossed to the window to look out. Bowen followed Ford and stood beside him.

Out in the street at the hitchrail, the horse provided by the town was now down and lying on its side.

Bowen's forehead furrowed. 'That's strange. I heard them say it would at least make it out of town.'

Ford gave him a sidelong glance and then looked back out at the dead animal. His mind was working overtime as he tried to figure out what he could do. Backing away from the window, he said, 'Tell me what else you overheard.'

'You better shut your mouth, scribbler, if you know what's good for you,' Hiram snarled.

'Pay him no never mind, Bowen.'

'Speak and you're dead,' Hiram snarled.

Ford's lips pressed together and he turned away from Bowen. He walked across to Hiram and ripped the man's bandanna from around his neck and forced it into his mouth.

Ford growled at him when he was finished. 'Keep it up and I'll knock you cold.'

Turning back, he said, 'Go on.'

'There's an issue with one of the brothers. I think his name is Cort. Apparently he used to be a sheriff's deputy up north somewhere. Hays City I think they said.'

'Yeah, so?'

Bowen's eyes grew wide as he continued, 'The old man didn't know. He treats his sons like excreta, just quietly.'

Ford frowned at the diversion from the story and the writer grimaced. He went on, 'They all thought he came straight back here from wherever he was. Which is technically true, but where he was, was Austin. He's a Texas Ranger. They sent him here to spy on his kinfolk.'

'Ain't that one for the books,' Ford said. 'I bet the old man took that well.'

'He tried to strike him down but Cort struck him instead. Then one of his brothers hit him from behind. They were going to lock him away in an upstairs room at the saloon while they dealt with you.'

Ford turned and looked at Hiram. 'You hear that? Your brother's a ranger.'

Hiram glared and said something that was muffled by the bandanna.

'What are you going to do?' Bowen asked.

'I have no idea.'

'You can't just leave him there. I believe they mean

to kill him.'

Ford thought for a moment and asked Bowen, 'Do you feel like starring in a book you ain't wrote yet?'

Fear crept across the man's face. 'I – ahh – I don't know. What would you have me do?'

'Nothing until after dark. How long have you been in town?'

Bowen frowned. 'A couple of days, why?'

'Do you know of a good place to hide a horse?'

Bowen looked at the roan and asked, 'Him?'

The horse snorted at the writer.

'Yeah, him. It looks like we might be hanging around town for a while and I need to hide him.'

The writer stood quietly for at least a minute while he thought, then his face changed and he pointed at the sky with an index finger. 'Yes, there's an old church on the edge of town which might do.'

Ford nodded. 'OK, we wait until dark then hide the horse there.'

A sudden change seemed to overcome Bowen and the writer became excited, eager to help. 'Is there anything else you want me to do now?'

Ford stared at Hiram and after a moment, looked about the room. He saw what he wanted and walked over to a barrel that had shovel handles in it. He took out four and then searched for something to cut them with. He found a small handsaw behind the counter.

Once that Ford had what he required, he gave them to Bowen.

'What do you want me to do with these?'

The deputy marshal walked over to Hiram and slipped a dynamite stick from behind the rope. He tossed it to Bowen. The poor man's eyes grew wide when he realized what it was. He dropped what he'd been holding, to catch the dynamite.

Fumbling it, he caught it then dropped it at his feet. Before it had touched the floorboards, Bowen had a finger in both ears and his eyes squeezed shut, waiting for the BANG!

When it never eventuated, he opened one eye and then the other. His chest heaved a huge sigh of relief.

Ford smiled at him. 'Cut them handles up the same length as that.'

'What are you going to do?'

Ford walked 'I'm going to get us another horse.'

It was Joe who broke the news about the horse. He ran into the saloon and said, 'Pa, we got a problem. The horse is dead.'

Charlie glowered at his son. 'Already?'

'Uh huh.'

Charlie was about to let loose a stream of invectives when the batwings flew back and Mart came storming in.

'Pa, we got us a problem.'

'Damn it, I know, Mart, the horse you got dropped dead too early.'

'I think he means me.'

Everyone in the room looked at Ford as he came through the batwings. Sawn-off shotgun in one hand, double hammers eared back, and the collar of Gray's shirt in the other as he pushed the man along before him.

Charlie Dent came to his feet. 'By Christ, you got you some big cajones on you, mister.'

'My horse is dead, I want another.'

'What's to stop me shooting you now?'

'For starters, I got me a shotgun pointed at your son,' Ford pointed out. 'And the other reason is that I still have Hiram.'

'But you are here, so I say shoot that son. He's useless to me anyway. We'll kill you and go and get Hiram.'

Alarm registered on Gray's face. 'Pa!'

'Before you go and do that, you might want to know your son ain't alone.'

Charlie smiled coldly at Ford. 'I wasn't born yesterday, Marshal. You're lying. There ain't no one over there.'

Ford started dragging Gray backward. 'Follow me.'

They went outside onto the boardwalk. The sun was sinking in the west and the few shadows that were left, stretched beyond all proportion.

'Can you hear me over there?' Ford shouted.

'I hear you loud and clear.'

Charlie frowned, puzzled.

'Now do you believe me?'

'Yeah, I believe you.'

'Good. Now, I want another horse. Actually, make it two. My friend will be needing one.'

'I'll have to get them from out of town,' Charlie said, trying to stall for time.

'That's fine. I changed my mind and wasn't planning on leaving until morning now, anyhow.'

The rancher nodded.

'Now, one other thing. If I turn and start walking back to the jail, none of your sons are going to try and shoot me down, are they?'

'Nope. You'll be given safe passage. For now.'

'Thank you.'

Ford let Gray go and turned away. He'd only just started across the street when a shot rang out. The hot passage of the slug past the deputy marshal's head told Ford how close it was. He went down on one knee, turned as he did so, and palmed up the Peacemaker.

'Hold it!' Charlie Dent boomed.

Ford was a hair away from killing the rancher who had stepped between Ford and Joe.

'I see your word ain't worth the breath it takes to give it,' Ford's voice was caustic.

'I'll deal with the boy. You keep going where you are. There'll be no more gunfire.'

And there wasn't. Ford made it back to the mining supplies store without further violation.

When Charlie saw the door close he whirled on Joe and struck him in the face with his fist. Joe sat down hard and looked up in bewilderment at his father. 'What did you do that for?'

'Because I gave the man my word, that's why.' Charlie looked around and saw Hogue. 'Hogue, find a couple of horses.'

'You ain't going to do that are you, Pa?' Gray

blurted out.

'We are going to do exactly what he wants. And tomorrow, when Jake has his Sharps, we'll finish this once and for all.'

Ford slammed the door behind him and said, 'We're getting out of here.'

'And go where?' Bowen asked incredulously.

'Once it's dark, we're moving to the cathouse down the street. While I take Hiram, you hide the horse. I'll need a distraction, so use two sticks of dynamite. Make them go bang on the outskirts of town. I'll put a decent fuse on the stuff so you have time to get away. Once you're done, I'll meet you at our destination. Now, let's get this dynamite changed over.'

'Where is it?'

'What?'

'The cat thingy.'

Ford sighed. 'Come here.'

Both men crossed to the window and Ford pointed the whorehouse out to him. 'See that there? The Pink Palace.'

'Oh good Lord. It's right next to the saloon. Where they are holed up.'

'It also gives me access to the first-floor balcony so I can get that ranger out of there. I ain't leaving without him.'

CHAPTER 5

'Hey, Joe, you know cousin Jeb had a back door to that place, don't you?'

Joe stared at Billy and nodded. 'Yeah, but it's all got crates against it, this high.' He held a hand palm down above the floor at neck level.

'Not anymore. How else do you think that other feller got in there? It wasn't through the front because I been watching it.'

Joe's eyes lit up. 'We should tell Pa.'

He turned to walk across to his father's table when Billy placed a hand on his arm to restrain him. 'Just hold on a minute there, brother. Let's think this through.'

'What do you mean?'

'If we're to go ahead and save old Hiram's ass from the marshal, I reckon Pa would look mighty favourable upon us.'

Joe shot his father a cautious glance. The rancher was back at his table, toying with the shot glass.

'I don't know, Billy,' Joe said. 'I think we should

tell him. He's going to get real mad if we don't.'

Billy shook his head. 'No, he won't. He'll be too happy that we got Hiram out of there.'

The batwings screeched and heads turned to see Jake walk into the saloon, his much treasured 'Big Fifty' Sharps in his hand.

'You're forgetting about him too,' Joe said, indicating his brother.

Charlie looked up at Jake and said, 'Good, you're back. Did you see Hogue?'

'Yeah, he told me what happened with the horse. And about Cort.'

Being the eldest of the brothers, Jake was the rancher's favourite. He was the one who'd take over the reins once the old man was gone.

He looked around the room. 'Where's Mart?'

'I'm here.'

Jake looked up at the head of the stairs to see his brother begin to descend. He waited in silence until Mart was in front of him. There was no love lost between these two. In fact, there was none lost between Jake and any of them. To the Dent brothers, Jake was their enemy. He was the one standing in their way of a stake in their father's empire.

'What do you want?'

The butt of the Sharps snapped forward and caught Mart in his midsection. The younger Dent doubled over as the air whooshed from his lungs. He then sank to his knees and gasped for air.

'Next time you might want to get it right when Pa asks you to do something,' Jake growled. He cast a defiant glance around the room to see if anyone would protest his actions.

There were none.

He stared at his father. 'Where's Cort?'

'Upstairs, locked away in a room.'

Jake put the Sharps on a scarred tabletop and walked towards the stairs, his stride purposeful. 'It's time me and him had us a little talk about where his loyalties lie.'

Loud stomps echoed around the dirty walls of the barroom as Jake ascended the steps. Once at the top, he disappeared along the hallway towards the rooms.

'I'd hate to be in your brother's boots right now, boys. Especially with Jake on the prod the way he is.'

Mart dragged himself up with the aid of a chair. The three sons stared at their father but said nothing.

The old man's eyes glowered. 'Why can't you all be more like Jake?'

More silence.

'Bah! I'm wasting my time.'

Charlie went back to his drink and brooded in silence.

Billy ushered Joe to one side. 'Well? Are you in or out?'

Joe gave his father a sidelong glance and set his jaw firm. 'Yeah, let's do it. We'll show the old son of a bitch we ain't as worthless as he seems to think.'

Cort was sitting on the edge of the bed when the door swung open and Jake filled the doorway. Outside it was now dark, and a decorative wall sconce was the room's only illumination. The room itself was small and consisted of the iron-framed bed, a wash-stand and dish, along with a chipped water jug, battered chair, and stained floor rug.

When Jake stepped into the room, Cort knew there was going to be trouble. Instead of waiting for it, however, he rose to meet his brother halfway.

The older Dent's face screwed up and he snarled, 'You traitorous son of a bitch.'

Cort said, 'You talk too much.' And with that, punched his brother in the mouth.

Jake was stunned by the blow. The last time the two had fought, Cort couldn't have knocked a sick person off a chamber pot. It was evident that he'd toughened up substantially during his absence.

Wiping the thin trickle of blood from the corner of his mouth, Jake smiled. 'Looks like you've hard-ened up some, little brother. Makes it more interesting.'

Once upon a time, Jake would have cut an impos-ing figure before Cort. Now he was no such thing. 'Get on with it, Jake. I ain't got all day.'

There was a hint of uncertainty in Jake's eyes as he closed in on his brother. Cort saw it and used it to his advantage. He moved with speed, delivering two swift blows to Jake's face. The older brother's head rocked back after each one landed.

Cort expected him to step away again, but he didn't. Instead, Jake let out an angry roar and charged.

Jake hit his brother hard with his right shoulder,

the momentum carrying them across the room and sending them crashing against a timber chair, which folded into matchwood with a resounding crash.

The broken chair arm dug into Cort's ribs, bringing forth a gasp of pain. He tried to roll left and dislodge his brother from on top, but Jake was substantially heavier and proved difficult to move. Pushing himself up a touch so that with a knee either side, he was astride Cort, Jake drove a hard punch into his brother's face, cutting the flesh of the cheek.

He pulled his arm back ready to land another blow when Cort's searching right hand grabbed a broken piece of chair and brought it up in a savage arc. With an audible crack, the timber laid solidly against Jake's head caused enough damage, creating an opportunity for Cort to push the heavier man away to his right.

They staggered to their feet, and once more, charged each other like two bull buffalo. A quick flurry of blows drew further blood from each man. A left from Jake knocked Cort back against the bed, while a right from Cort caused his brother to stagger into the washstand. The jug and dish fell to the floor and shattered, water splashing on to the rug.

They drew back from each other, their breathing ragged. Both sucked in deep breaths before they went back to it.

'You had enough yet, Jake?'

'I got plenty left in me that'll help wail the tar outta a traitor like you, Cort.'

The younger Dent wiped some of the blood from

his face. 'Hiram and Billy killed two marshals, Jake. It ain't going to stop after you kill another. Now the rangers are involved too.'

Jake sneered at Cort. 'The problem is, little brother, if the marshal takes in Hiram and Billy, it won't be long before they come looking for me.'

Cort frowned at first, not sure what his sibling meant. Then: 'You were behind it? The killing of the marshals?'

'Sure I was. I killed the first one who came snooping around looking for Hiram. The second one, I was busy doing something else so I had Abel tell Billy and Hiram to take care of it.'

'Did Pa order you to do it?'

Jake snorted derisively. 'Silly old fool thinks that Billy and Hiram were behind the whole thing. They didn't say nothing, though. They ain't brave enough.'

'So I'm next, is that it?'

Jake nodded. 'That was the plan, but you seem to have toughened up some, Cort. Once Pa is gone I could use you to run things. And keep the others in line.'

Cort thought it was some kind of joke at first. But then he saw his brother's eyes. 'You're serious?'

'Damned right I am. What do you say? I'd rather have you beside me than have to kill you, Cort.'

The younger brother looked around the room as though considering the offer. He opened his mouth to speak, when the distant sound of gunfire filled the night air.

Jake cursed and the six-gun on his right hip leaped into his hand. He held it on Cort and snapped, 'You stay here. I'll expect an answer when I get back.'

With that, Jake backed out the door and closed and locked it behind him.

'Get me another bottle, Harry, would you?' Charlie called over to the barkeep. 'This one kinda dried up.'

Mart and Gray sat with their father. Billy and Joe had disappeared. Jake was still upstairs with Cort, and his remaining hands were outside.

The batwings swung open and a thin woman in a blue dress entered, carrying a tray of biscuits. 'I figured you could use these, Charlie. It ain't a proper meal, but it's something.'

'Thank you, Maude, that's right kind of you.'

Maude was Charlie's sister-in-law, and although no one could understand why, had a soft spot for him.

She'd just placed the tray on the table when the sound of a shotgun going off in the distance made her jump. The throaty roar was preceded by a couple of shots from a six-gun.

Charlie came to his feet and stared at the door. He looked around the room and then back at Gray and Mart. 'Where are your brothers?'

They shrugged.

'Ah hell, no,' Charlie groaned.

He was about to make for the batwings when Jake thundered down the stairs.

'Jake, I think it's your brothers. I think it's Joe and Billy.'

A snarled expression came across Jake's face. 'Stupid bastards.'

The four men hurried outside on to the board-walk. Charlie looked at one of his hands and snapped, 'What's going on?'

'It came from around the back of the store, Mr Dent.'

'C'mon,' Jake said, and stepped down onto the street.

They were headed for a side alley when Joe came stumbling out of the darkness into the light cast by the lantern outside the saloon. He was covered in blood from his head down to his waist. One look was enough to tell them that something had gone awfully wrong.

Alarm registered on Charlie Dent's face. 'Joe, where's your brother?'

Joe stared into the distance as he started to walk past his father. Charlie reached out and grabbed him. 'Joe?'

Joe's eyes came back into focus. 'Oh, hi, Pa.'

'Where's your brother, Joe? Where's Billy?'

'He's dead, Pa. Billy's dead.'

Charlie Dent looked toward the mining supplies store, his face displaying the shock he felt at learning of his son's demise.

And then the store blew up, spraying the street with a hail of wooden splinters.

Those inside the mining supplies store were about to leave when the door in the rear room squeaked on stiff hinges. Bowen was about to say something, but

Ford held a finger to his own lips to quiet him.

The deputy marshal eased back the hammers on the sawn-off shotgun in his hands, and moved silently across the floor to the opening which led into the back room.

No sooner had he shown himself than the store filled with the thunder of guns. Billy fired first, a wild shot that flew to Ford's left and punched through the paper-thin wall.

The shotgun roared and the double charge of buckshot almost cut Billy Dent in half. Blood sprayed across Joe who was behind his brother. It caused him to panic and he fired three shots in Ford's general direction without hitting anything.

Ford dropped the shotgun and palmed up his Peacemaker. He fired at Joe who was now fleeing through the rear door. The slugs from Ford's Colt dug splinters from the door frame as the young man disappeared.

'Marshal! You have a problem!'

It was Bowen, and from the sound of his voice, whatever it was, it had to be bad.

Ford rushed back into the storefront and found Bowen crouched over Hiram Dent. 'What happened?'

'He was hit by a bullet that came through the wall,' there was urgency in his voice. 'I think it was a good idea you swapped the dynamite when you did.'

Ford checked him out. It was obvious that the killer had been hit hard. Under normal circumstances, Ford would have left him there to die. But the situation wasn't normal and he needed Hiram alive.

'Help me get him up, Bowen, hurry.'

The writer helped Ford free the wounded young man from the rope and got Hiram over his shoulder. Then Ford said, 'Take the horse and hide him.'

'What are you going to do?'

'Make this place go bang so I can get to the cathouse with Hiram. I'll meet you there.'

Bowen went to take up the roan's reins when the animal pulled back and made to bite.

'You do and I'll blow you up with this place,' Ford warned the animal. 'Get out of here.'

Thirty seconds later they were gone.

With Hiram still over his shoulder, Ford lit the fuse to a stick of dynamite and then scooped up his Winchester. That done, he hurried out the back door.

As soon as the store blew, he rushed across the dusty street amidst all the confusion and men as they ducked for cover. He slipped down a side alley and around the rear of the building. From there he found the back door and stomped up the steps. He tried the doorknob, and when the door sprang free, he walked inside.

Ford found himself at the end of a long carpeted hallway and began walking along it when a door on the left opened.

After a brief hesitation, he brought the Winchester up and waited to see who would emerge. It was a woman dressed in a red corset with black lace trimmings and black underwear. The blast must have drawn her attention because she was in the middle of putting on a red dressing-gown. She gasped when she saw Ford standing there with Hiram over his shoulder, the rifle pointed in her direction.

'Who are you?'

'Ford, United States Deputy Marshal.'

Her eyes widened with recognition. 'You're him.'

'Yeah, I'm him. Who are you?'

'Gracey. This is my place,' she said.

Gracey was tall, slim, had black hair, and from what he saw before she closed her gown, was well formed. It was hard to tell in the dim light of the hall, but he figured her to be of similar age to him.

'Are you a Dent?'

She chuckled. 'Good Lord, no. You won't find anyone by the name of Dent working here.'

'Good, this feller is getting heavy . . .'

Her eyes widened again and she indicated the room from which she'd emerged. 'Yes, follow me, you can put him in here. Is that Hiram?'

'Yes, and I'd rather he goes upstairs.'

'Only the girls' working rooms are upstairs,' Gracey told him.

'Good. Lead the way.'

Gracey thought to protest but instead nodded and said, 'Follow me.'

They walked along the hall to the far end and stopped before a door, which was ajar. She held up her hand and peered through the gap, then waved to someone on the other side and pushed the timber door wider to let the person through.

Another woman. Red-haired, thin, medium-built, and unlike Gracey, no gown. She opened her mouth to speak when she sighted Ford. 'Oh my God, you're him.'

Ford rolled his eyes. 'Yeah. . . .'

'Gracey, he blew up the mining supplies store.'

'What?' She turned to look at him.

'That was the explosion just before. There's nothing left. Except for junk.'

'Listen,' Ford snapped impatiently. 'Help me get this killer upstairs and I'll answer all of your questions then. OK?'

The two women nodded.

'I'm going to need a doctor, too. Preferably someone who can be trusted.'

'There's only one,' Gracey said. 'You'll be able to trust him.'

She turned her gaze to the redhead. 'May, go and get Rosie. Tell her to find the doctor and tell no one else about it. Have her bring him to your room.'

'Sure, Gracey.'

May disappeared and Gracey turned back to Ford. 'Follow me.'

The doorway opened into a large, empty foyer. The floor was totally covered with carpet. Against the far wall were twin lounges and a hardwood desk. The walls were wood panelled, and from the ceiling hung an ornate chandelier. On the walls were five paintings of naked ladies reclining in various positions.

There were twin doors at the entrance, their

stained-glass sections at head height, and a large staircase that curved around to the right with a hand-carved balustrade.

'Business is booming,' Ford commented.

'What can I say? Dents pay well.'

On cue, Hiram moaned.

They started up the stairs, and once at the top, were met by a young blonde woman in a plain blue dress. She stared at Ford and then said to Gracey, 'I'll be as quick as I can.'

'Be careful, Rosie, you know what the Dents can be like.'

Ford followed Gracey along another hall until she stopped at a doorway, second to last on the right. She opened the door and stepped aside. May was there waiting for them, the blankets on her double bed pulled back.

Ford placed Hiram on the mattress and stood back while May began to undress him. He looked at Gracey. 'You'll need to keep an eye out for a feller called Bowen. He'll be along directly.'

Gracey nodded and said, 'I'll take care of it.'

'Thank you. And thanks for putting us up here until things quiet down a piece.'

Gracey's lips set in a thin line and she said, 'I figure I don't have much of a choice. Something about you told me you were coming in whether I said yes or no. Right now I'd best get back downstairs, just in case Charlie and his brood come knocking on my door. The window over there overlooks the street, so you'll be able to keep a watch out for what's going on.'

She turned to leave when Ford stopped her. 'Before you go, what do you know about Cort Dent?'

Gracey's expression took a dramatic change. She looked at Ford with fire in her eyes and said bitterly, 'I know that if he ever steps foot in here, I'll kill the son of a bitch.'

Ford opened his mouth to speak when a shout came up from the street below. One so piercing that even the closed window stood no chance of keeping it out.

'Marshal! I'm going to kill you, Marshal! You killed my Billy, you son of a bitch!'

Ford looked at Gracey. 'You killed one of his sons?'

He shrugged. 'Seems to me he's having a bad day.'

'And your night is about to get a lot worse.'

'Only if he finds me.'

May said, 'He'll turn this town upside down to find you. Him and his kin.'

'He's kind of short on a few of them now, too. Someone named Joey, another named Jeb, and three or so others.'

Sarcasm dripped from Gracey's voice when she said, 'Keep this up and there'll be no Dents left. They'll have to change the name of the town to Undamaged.'

Ford gave her a wry smile. 'I like that.'

'Did you hear me, Ford? I'm going to turn this town upside down until I find you!'

Both women stared at Ford. He shrugged his shoulders. 'Looks like there's going to be some more Dents need straightening out.'

CHAPTER 6

'I'm telling you, Jake, the only ones in there is Billy and Jeb.'

Jake stared at Mart before turning and walking over to his father. 'They're not there, Pa. It's . . . Mart said the only one there was Billy.'

The old man glared at his son. 'Turn this place over until you find them, Jake. They can't have got out of town yet. Which means they're hiding out somewhere. Find that damned marshal and the one who helped him. Then bring them to me. I want them to pay for what happened to Billy.'

'Sure, Pa.'

'And don't let nothing happen to Hiram. Make sure.'

Jake nodded. He looked about. 'Have you seen Joe?'

'He's over at the saloon.'

'OK. I'll be right back.'

'Where are you going?' Charlie demanded.

'Just to have a talk to Joe. He might've seen something.'

Jake hurried over to the saloon and walked inside. He saw Joe sitting at a corner table with a bottle of whiskey in front of him. He set a course for the table and weaved through the chairs until he stood before his brother.

'Get up and come with me,' Jake said in a menacing tone.

There was a nervousness to Joe's eyes when he looked up at his brother's grim face. 'Why?'

'Just do it.'

Joe glanced around the room. 'I . . . ahh, I'm right here.'

Jake firmed the set of his jaw, walked around the table and grabbed a handful of Joe's greasy dark hair. He then rammed the head forehead first into the table, stunning him. There was a loud bang as the hard bone met the wooden tabletop, followed by a yelp of pain and a moan.

Without waiting, Jake dragged him to his feet and the chair was knocked over in the process. He then hauled Joe across the barroom under the watchful eye of those who remained inside.

'Quit it, Jake.'

'Shut up, Joe.'

When they reached the door to the back room, Jake drew back his foot and gave it a solid kick. It smashed back, and Jake dragged his brother inside. He let go of his hair and turned to slam the door.

Joe gathered himself and cursed, 'Son of a bitch, Jake, what did you go and do that for?'

The older Dent brother turned back and moved

towards the younger one. Joe's eyes widened. 'Hang on a minute, Jake.'

His protest did him no good. Once Jake was within reach, he cocked his fist and drove it into his brother's jaw.

Joe sprawled across the floor. He lay there stunned for a moment but soon started squirming when Jake hauled him to his feet once more.

'Hold it, Jake. What are you doing?'

Another blow and Joe crashed down again. This time, however, Jake stepped forward and kicked him in the side. A loud grunt escaped Joe's lips and his brother leaned down and dragged him to his feet again.

'What the hell were you and Billy thinking?' Jake snarled.

'He said we could get Pa to take us more serious if we could get Hiram back,' Joe gasped as he climbed to his feet.

'You're an idiot. Both of you. Now Billy is dead, and Jeb too.'

Joe gave his brother a sullen look. 'It weren't meant to go that way.'

'Yeah, well, it did. Now get out there and search the town for the marshal and Hiram. They couldn't have got out of town because the roads have people on them.'

The doctor arrived around thirty minutes after they'd put Hiram into May's bed. He was a serious-looking man in his early forties, wore glasses, his hair was thinning on top, and he had a medium build.

After he'd finished examining Hiram he stared at Ford and said, 'He'll be dead before the sun comes up.'

Ford cursed under his breath. 'Isn't there anything you can do for him?'

'Not in this lifetime.'

'Thanks, Doc.'

The medico stared at Ford for a moment before saying, 'If I were you, I'd cut my losses and get out of town right smart.'

'That's just it, Doc. You ain't me.'

The man shrugged and left the room.

Gracey looked at Ford. 'It was sound advice, you know.'

'It probably was. But I can't leave until I do two more things.'

'Such as?'

'Jake Dent was the one behind the deaths of the two previous marshals who came here, not his old man. Although I'm guessing I'll still have to deal with him.'

'And the second?'

'Cort Dent.'

Anger flared in Gracey's eyes. 'That son of a bitch.'

Ford shot her a questioning look. 'What is it with you and him? Didn't he pay or something?'

'Mind your own damned business,' Gracey snapped, then turned and stormed from the room.

He shook his head. 'Good one, Josh.'

Oh, well. He couldn't worry about hurt feelings

just at that point. He was trapped in a town where every second person wanted to kill him, there was a ranger to rescue, and his prisoner was about to breathe his last. On top of that, there was Jake Dent.

Just maybe it would be best to cut his losses and live to fight another day when the odds were substantially more favourable.

'What did your brother have to say for himself?'

'He says they were doing it to impress you.'

Charlie Dent rolled his eyes. 'Did I raise nothing but fools? Damn it, I swear, near every one of you takes after your mother's side of the family.'

'Well, they can't get out of town. We've got it sewn up.'

'You want to hope so. If they get out of this town, I'm going to take the bullwhip to every one of you.'

Bowen returned around the same time that Hiram Dent breathed his last. May showed him into the room where Ford and Gracey stood over the newly deceased body. It was almost midnight and the search was still well underway for the fugitives.

'That doesn't look too good,' Bowen said.

Ford nodded. 'You could say that.'

'Where to from here, Marshal Ford?'

'I've one more thing to do, and then we'll be leaving.'

Gracey raised her eyebrows. 'You're leaving? Not without me, you ain't. As soon as they find out I helped you, I'm done.'

Ford stared at her. 'What?'

'I said . . .'

'I heard what you said.'

'Well, you ain't. May and Rosie will be coming too.'

Ford shook his head. 'We'll be lucky to get out of here *without* you along. It's too dangerous. Besides, I'll be back. I ain't done with this place by a long shot.'

'What about the swamp?' Gracey asked. 'That's the last place they would think we'd go.'

Don't go into the swamp.

'I don't know anything about the swamp,' Ford pointed out.

'Cort does.'

Don't go into the swamp.

'Shit.'

Ford stared at Bowen. 'It looks like you're about to become a horse thief.'

The marshal was expecting a look of apprehension to appear on Bowen's face. Instead, there was one of excitement. 'Tell me what to do.'

'Get them from the livery. Then put them with my horse. Once I get Cort out of the saloon, we'll all be along.'

Bowen nodded.

'One other thing. Don't get caught or they'll kill you,' Ford warned him. He turned to Gracey. 'I'm going to need a distraction.'

'What kind of a distraction?' she asked.

'One that'll get heads turning the other way while I jump across to the other balcony.'

She gave him a sly smile. 'I can do that. Give me a couple of minutes.'

She left the room with Bowen, and Ford walked across to the window. He waited for a moment before opening it. Then he stepped through and out on to the balcony. He slid along the wall to the railing on the saloon side. There was about an eight-foot gap between the two and he knew what it would take to negotiate the crossing.

There were voices from down in the street and he saw Gracey walk out into the middle of it. She deftly glanced up to the balcony and saw Ford.

Then something happened that gave Ford reason to pause. Gracey's dress slipped off, and she was standing in the middle of the street in her bloomers. Naked from the waist up. Then she held up her left hand. In it was a bottle of whiskey.

She called out at the top of her voice and started to dance. Twirling around, singing out loud, giggling. Men began to gather, all eyes on her.

As Gracey spun around again, she looked up and saw Ford staring down. A fleeting angry expression crossed her face long enough for Ford to get the message and refocus on the job at hand.

He tightened his grip on the Winchester and ran at the far balustrade. As soon as he reached it, he jumped up with one big stride. His right boot placed on the rail, he launched himself across the gap and landed on the other side.

Ford glanced down at Gracey and saw her surrounded by ogling men. She looked up and saw that he'd made it. Her job done, she slapped one of the men across the face, which drew a howl of guffaws from the others. She then stomped her foot, picked up her dress, and stormed back inside her establishment.

The balcony ran all the way along the front of the saloon so Ford knew he needed to be careful. Pick the room with no light was the best bet. So, he did.

He eased the window open, stepped on through and started to pad across the room towards the light he could see beneath the base of the closed door.

'I'll give you ten seconds to tell me what you're doing before I blow your damned fool head off,' growled a deep voice.

'Just passing through, friend,' Ford said.

'Funny way to be passing through,' the man said. 'I got me one of them theory things.'

The room was dark enough that the only thing Ford could see was a large lump in the bed.

'Well, hurry up and spit it out because there's something I have to do.'

'I figure you're going to break out that feller they got tied up in the next room. Am I right?'

'Maybe.'

The man swung out of bed. 'Good.'

'What are you doing?' Ford asked, puzzled.

'I'm going to help.'

'You what?'

The man started to dress. 'The name's Isaiah White, and if I don't miss my guess, you'd be that marshal feller, Ford, they're all talking about.'

'I ain't got time for this, White.'

'My next guess is that you're going to be headed for the swamp. Only way you might have a chance of getting out. Am I right?'

'Yes, damn it.'

'Good, then you need me. I grew up in the swamps. I know a lot of trails that others don't. So, I'm coming. You need my help.'

'Why?'

'I don't like Charlie Dent and his brood.'

'What about the one in the next room?'

'Cort? I hear tell he's a ranger. I changed my opinion of that one.'

White had finished and was dressed. He picked up a rifle from beside his bed and Ford realized that when he'd entered the room, the man hadn't been armed.

'Well, come on, let's go get him. What are you waiting for?'

Ford shook his head. Could it get any worse?

CHAPTER 7

The hallway was well lit but empty. Ford slipped out of the doorway with his Colt in his fist, ready to fire at whatever target presented itself, his Winchester at his side. He eased himself along the wall, White behind him. In the light, he finally got a better look at the man who wanted to help.

White was unshaven, had long hair, and was every bit of six feet tall. He wore ragged clothes and sported no six-gun, just the rifle. Before Ford entered the room, he said to White, 'Keep an eye out. I'll be a few moments. You see a Dent, fix him.'

Ford tried the handle but the door was locked. He looked back at White, and said 'I hate to do this.'

He drew back his right leg, and with all the force he could generate, drove his boot heel against the door. Wood splintered from the frame and the door itself flew back with a crash. Ford stepped into the room and saw Cort sitting on the bed.

'Come on,' Ford snapped. 'I'm getting you out of here.'

Cort Dent didn't need to be told twice. He came off the bed and moved with stiff strides towards the doorway.

'Who are you?' Cort asked.

'Ford.'

'The marshal? The one who's been raining down hell on this fair town?'

Ford grunted. 'I'm sorry about your kin.'

'Don't let that worry you. Whatever they got, they deserved.'

'You fellers done with your howdy-dos in there?' White asked. 'If you are, we're about to have company.'

Ford gave Cort his Winchester and they moved out into the hallway. At that same time, a figure appeared at the far end, at the top of the stairs.

Ford squeezed off a shot and the man was flung back against the wall. Ford didn't wait to see what happened next, but instead, turned and followed the others into White's room. The three of them emerged on to the balcony and looked around. Behind them, they could hear footsteps and shouts as their pursuers got closer.

'What now, Marshal?' White asked, a touch of sarcasm in his voice.

'Over the edge,' Ford snapped and climbed over the balustrade.

Before the other two men had made it halfway, he'd dropped to the ground.

White and Cort Dent landed beside him, the former grunting after a hard landing. A shout from within the saloon drew attention to them, and the batwings burst open.

Charlie Dent stood there like a giant sequoia. He saw the man who'd killed his boys, and the son he wished he'd never had, as they stood there together on the street. His face turned into a snarl and he brought up a six-gun in his hand. 'Now you'll pay, you son of a bitch.'

Before Ford could react, the Winchester in Cort's hands fired. Orange flame belched from the gun's muzzle and the elder Dent staggered as the slug punched into his chest. Cort levered and fired again, the second bullet slamming home not far from the first.

Charlie dropped to his knees, shoulders slumped.

'Pa!' a voice shouted and Gray Dent appeared behind his father. He saw the fugitives before him and cursed. Fighting to bring his own gun into line, he was stopped dead when a .45 slug from Ford's Peacemaker hit him flush in the chest. Gray Dent was dead before he hit the floor behind his father.

Immediately, the large front window of the Dent Saloon exploded outwards on to the boardwalk as a hail of bullets tore through it.

Behind them, more men spilled from the saloon and fired shot after shot. At their head was Jake Dent.

'Kill them! Don't let them get away!'

More gunfire rocked the main street of Dent. Ford swivelled and fired a round from his Peacemaker. It missed the older Dent, and instead slammed into Mart, one of his two remaining brothers.

'I'm hit, Jake!' he exclaimed. 'I'm . . .'

A second slug from the Colt cut him short as it hammered into his forehead.

Jake fired wildly at his brother Cort, but his bullets whipped past the ranger without striking home. Then Joe Dent gave a wild yell at the sight of his fallen father, and fanned the hammer of his six-gun uselessly. His bullets went everywhere except at their intended target, and it gave White time to sight and fire.

Joe Dent went up on to his toes as the slug burned deep. A second slug from White, and Joe Dent's life came to a violent end.

That left Jake Dent. He stood there, still firing, eyes rolling wildly in his head, a snarl etched on his face as he fired again at his traitorous brother.

A slug clipped Cort in the shoulder and spun him around. Jake cried out with glee and drew back the hammer for the killing shot. But he was suddenly thrown back as the Peacemaker in Ford's fist crashed and the bullet smashed into his chest.

The deputy marshal fired again and put the last of the wild Dent brothers down.

The thunder of gunfire died away, but the three men in the street held their guns ready just in case. Then the batwings swung open and an unarmed Hogue Polsen emerged.

'I ain't got a gun, Cort.'

'You're under arrest, Hogue,' Cort told him.

Ford said, 'I reckon we're done here. No need to go into the swamp after all, now.'

Ford tightened the cinch on the blue roan before turning to face Cort. 'Will you be all right here cleaning things up?'

Cort nodded. 'Yeah. Without the old man, they'll toe the line.'

He shifted his gaze to Gracey. 'You never did tell me what you and him was fighting about.'

She moved forward and kissed the deputy marshal on the cheek. 'Maybe one day I will.'

Suddenly Bowen appeared with a bay horse. 'I'm ready,' he said in a jovial voice.

'For what?'

'To come with you, of course.'

'Oh, no. You tag along with someone else.'

Bowen looked disappointed as he watched Ford climb aboard the roan. 'But . . .'

'No buts. You've haunted me enough already. Go write a story about a ranger.'

Cort held up a hand. 'I have no wish to be famous. Bye, Josh.'

Ford said, 'I'll be seeing you.' And then he turned the roan and eased him into a trot.

'You old son of a bitch, you set me up! Again!' Ford fumed at Grimes.

'I see you're back,' Grimes said.

'Yeah. No thanks to you,' Ford snapped. 'You might have told me that two marshals had gone there before me. And one of them happened to be your son.'

Grimes nodded and seemed weary all of a sudden. He walked across to his chair, sat down, and stared at Ford. 'What happened to Dent?'

'He's dead. They're all dead. But by Christ they did their best to put me in the ground.'

Surprise registered on the old marshal's face. 'You killed them all?'

'I had some help from a Texas ranger by the name of Cort Dent.'

Surprise registered on Grimes' face. He nodded. 'You're right. I should have told you. But I wanted revenge on that scum so bad I could taste it. I'm sorry, Josh. I used you because Bass said you were good.'

'Yes, you did, damn it.'

'I figured I had to keep it quiet. Would you have gone if I'd told you?'

Ford's gaze softened. 'Yes, I would. All you had to do was ask.'

'I'm sorry, son.'

A drawn-out silence ensued before Grimes opened his desk drawer. He took out a piece of paper and held it out. 'This came for you the other day.'

'What is it?' Ford asked, taking it.

'No idea.'

Ford unfolded it and read. He pondered over it when he had finished, and then screwed it up into a tight ball.

'What is it, Josh?'

'Bass has disappeared.'

'What?'

'According to this he was on a job and just vanished.'

'What are you going to do?'

'I'll head back north and see if I can find him.'

Grimes snorted.

Ford frowned. 'What?'

'Ever since you got here, all you've done is gripe about your pa and how he was an ornery son of a bitch. And yet you're willing to drop everything to go after him.'

Ford nodded. 'We may have our differences, and yes, he is a son of a bitch, but he's still my pa, and I'd walk through Hell itself to bring him back.'

PART 2

WHATEVER IT TAKES!

CHAPTER 8

Two Weeks Later

The Sundown Saloon in Bender's Gulch, Montana, was, as far as saloons went, reasonable in every way. The furnishings were nice, the liquor was good, the prices acceptable, and the whores still had all their teeth. Ford sat at a corner table with a half-empty bottle in front of him, his glass all but full. A whore whom he knew as Sandy, came up to him and asked 'Can I get you anything, Marshal?'

He shook his head, 'Not at the moment.'

'Suit yourself.'

She left Ford to himself, and ten minutes later, the main door swung open and a man he recognized entered. The newcomer glanced around and spotted Ford at the table. He started across the room, weaving in and out of the tables as he went.

Sitting across from Ford, he nodded. 'Josh. You made good time.'

'Ben. Any news on Bass?'

Lanky Ben Travers shook his head. 'Nothing yet.'

'Why are we meeting here then?'

'It's what the note said.'

Ford stared at him. 'I thought you said there was nothing new.'

'That's right. All we got was a note to come here and have you here, too.'

'Then tell me what you do know.'

'Bass was working a rustling case over near Rock Flats. He informed us when he arrived, but since then, there has been nothing.'

'How long ago was that.'

'Just after he sent you to Texas.'

'Hell, Ben! That was almost two months ago. Did anyone go looking for him?'

'I did. Came up empty. The folks there remember him showing up, and then he wasn't there any more.'

Movement across the room caught Ford's eye, and he saw the barkeep coming towards their table. The man stopped and held out a piece of paper. 'Feller gave me this to give to you. Said it was for you, *only.*'

Ford frowned and took the paper. He unfolded it and read. Once he had finished he handed it to Travers, who read it for himself.

He looked up at Ford and said, 'This is crazy.'

Ford nodded. 'It is.'

'Surely you can't be considering it?'

'Do you see any other choice? At least we know Bass is still alive,' he stared up at the barkeep. 'Who gave it to you?'

The man shrugged. 'Don't know. Never seen him before. Wore a suit, all neat and proper.'

'OK, thanks.'

The barkeep left, and Travers said, 'You can't go into Crazy Woman Hollow alone.'

'That's what it says. Go to Crazy Woman Hollow and brace Scar Ferguson.'

'Damn it, Ford. That son of a bitch is a killer. How do they know he's even there?'

'And if I don't go, they'll kill Bass. I'm going and that's it.'

'Whatever it takes?'

'Yeah. Whatever it takes.'

'Then I'm going too. I'll leave before you do and already be there when you arrive.'

Ford thought about it for a moment and nodded. 'OK. It may be for the best.'

'When are you going to leave?'

'In the morning.'

'I'll see you there.'

Crazy Woman Hollow sat between two large tree-covered hills and stank like the cesspool it was. Killings were a daily occurrence, along with gun-fights, fistfights, drinking and whoring. No respectable person would ever be seen in such a place, dead or alive.

The mean-tempered blue roan snorted his disgust as he started along the main street. At first he baulked, but a few stern words from Ford had him moving again.

The town was a mix of solid false-fronts, and false-fronts with canvas walls. The main thoroughfare was churned and muddy from a recent rainstorm that had passed over, dumping a heavy fall.

As the deputy marshal made his way along the street, a door crashed back on a rundown place with a sign above its door. It read Casino. A man staggered out and stopped. He ran his drunken gaze over the rider who was passing. On the man's shirt was pinned a star. Ford could hazard a guess how he got it. And he'd bet a month's pay it wasn't put there.

He suddenly became aware of his own badge, tucked away in his pocket. No point riding into a town like this with it advertising the fact that he was the law. It would only serve as a shiny target.

Ford found what he was looking for: a saloon, called simply Crazy Woman Saloon. At the hitch-rail out front, he recognized Travers' horse. He eased the roan in beside it and dismounted. He rubbed the horse on its muscular neck and said, 'Behave yourself.'

The animal snorted and turned its head to look at its rider. Ford nodded, saying 'I'll be back.'

Inside, the air was thick with a combination of odours. Sweat, smoke, vomit, stale alcohol. It all blended into one and assailed the nostrils.

Ford started to push through the crowd when he was approached by a whore. She wore corset and pantaloons. Both had once been white but were now a stained colour that resembled bleached bones. Her hair was a tangled red mess and her skin was pale and bruised.

'Hey, cowboy. Buy me a drink, or something else.'
She smiled and revealed blackened teeth.

The deputy marshal almost cringed. Instead, he gathered himself and said, 'Maybe later. I need to find Scar Ferguson.'

Alarm registered on her face. 'Are you the law?'

'Nope.'

'I ain't seen him.'

'I told you, I ain't the law.'

'I don't care, I ain't seen him.'

'Uh huh.'

Leaving her there, he walked up to the bar, then turned around so that he faced the room. At the top of his voice he shouted: 'I'm looking for a yellow son of a bitch named Scar Ferguson!'

The room went silent instantly, just shut down. Then came the shuffle of feet as the crowd parted to reveal an unshaven man no more than fifteen feet away. He was dressed in black, like Ford, but he had twin six-guns while the deputy marshal only had the one.

When the killer spoke, his voice was deep. 'Sounds to me like you're eager to be buried, *hombre*. Who are you?'

'The name's Josh Ford.'

A ripple ran through the crowd.

'Seems to me I heard of you.'

Who hadn't? After all, Ford had a reputation for getting the hard jobs done. He was like the marshals' best of the best.

'Most folks have.'

'I guess they'll be hearing about your death real soon, too.'

Ford let his right arm dangle, so his hand was near the butt of the Peacemaker. 'Let's see, shall we?'

Ferguson gave Ford a cold smile. 'See you in Hell, lawdog.'

Hands blurred, and guns flashed up. However, only one of them roared. The Peacemaker in Ford's fist crashed out and the .45 calibre slug burned deep into Scar Ferguson's chest. He lurched back, the six-gun in his hand still pointed at the floor.

Ford eared back the hammer on his own weapon once more and the killer before him gave him a bewildered look. The Peacemaker roared again, and Ferguson fell back against a table. It flipped over under his weight and landed on its edge beside the dead man.

Before the rumblings in the crowd could start, the deputy marshal moved the Colt back and forth over them. 'No one else moves unless you want to get buried beside Ferguson there.'

'He can't kill us all!' shouted an invisible man inside the crowd. 'Get him!'

They'd just started to surge forward when a gunshot sounded and stopped them dead. 'All of you hold it there!'

They turned to look at the other stranger who'd arrived earlier that day. He too had his six-gun out and had fired a round into the ceiling.

'I believe you folks were told what would happen if you tried anything,' Travers said. 'I do believe the next shot that is fired will kill whoever it hits.'

Travers started to make his way through the crowd

to stand beside Ford.

'Time to leave,' he observed.

'You could say that. Let's go.'

Travers stood in the doorway and covered the angry mob as they spilled out, while Ford mounted, then Ford did the same for Travers.

'You ready?' Ford asked.

'Yeah.'

'Let's ride.'

Heartbeats later, they were thundering along the dusty road out of town with the crowd shouting angrily after them.

Travers poked at the small fire with a stick. Flames leaped into the air, and small embers floated skyward with the almost invisible smoke.

'What do we do now?' he asked Ford.

The deputy marshal shrugged. 'Damned if I know. I guess we'll have to wait and see.'

'Head back to Bender's Gulch?'

'Maybe.'

'Or you could wait here,' a voice said from out of the dark.

Both men dropped hands to their weapons which came clear of leather.

A tall man in a suit stepped into the circle of fire-light. 'Take it easy, gentlemen. I'm just the messenger. Mind you, Marshal, you sure know how to handle yourself. Scar Ferguson didn't stand a chance.'

'Who the hell are you?' Ford snapped.

The man smiled. 'Like I said, I'm just the messenger.'

'Name and message,' Ford demanded.

The man reached into a pocket and retrieved a piece of paper. He passed it to Ford and said, 'The name is Bennett.'

The deputy marshal moved closer to the fire and opened the slip of paper and read through it.

'It's a list of names,' Bennett supplied. 'The whereabouts of the first on the list is the only one that's known. It's up to you to find the rest.'

'What am I supposed to do when I find them?'

'Why, kill them, of course.'

Travers snorted. 'You're kidding.'

Bennett shook his head. 'No. Not in the least. If you fail in your task, you'll never see your father again.'

Ford snapped, 'Get out of here before I kill you first.'

'An unwise move.'

'Go!'

The darkness quickly swallowed the retreating form of Bennett, and once he was gone, Travers said, 'You ain't considering this, are you?'

'Not much choice. I'll track each individual and decide on the course of action to take at that point in time.'

'Hell, Josh.'

'I'll give you a copy of these names, Ben. I want you to find out how they are connected.'

'All right. I'll do what I can.'

'If we attack this from both sides I think we'll be able to solve it and find Bass before they kill him.'

'How do I get word to you?'

'Don't unless you really need to. If you do, do it through Helena. They get wind we're on to them it might go bad for Bass.'

'I still don't like it, Josh.' Travers rubbed his chin while deep in thought.

Ford nodded. 'If you saw the first name on the list, you'd like it even less.'

'Who is it?'

'Elijah Thomas.'

Travers' eyes sprang wide. 'Isn't he. . . ?'

'Yeah. He's in Hardrock Pen.'

CHAPTER 9

The Hardrock Penitentiary sat on the banks of the Hardrock River. Its outer walls were made of large blocks of stone and rose at least twenty feet into the air. Guard towers were situated on each corner, and heavily-armed guards roamed the parapets.

The main gate was made of iron and clanged loudly as it closed once Ford had ridden through on the roan.

He rode the horse across to a hitch rail outside the warden's office and dismounted.

'Can I help you, Marshal Ford?'

Ford turned and faced a thin guard. 'I want to see the warden. Is he in?'

'Yes, sir. Follow me.'

Ford brushed trail dust from his pants, and went inside, waiting in the outer office while the guard announced him. When the man reappeared, he said, 'Warden Bromley will see you now.'

Ford walked through to the inner sanctum of the warden's office and the guard closed the door behind him. Bromley sat behind his desk. He was a large, round man in his forties with a receding hair-line.

'Marshal Ford. What is it I can do for you?'

'Warden, I need to speak with one of your prison-ers.'

'Which one?'

'Elijah Thomas.'

Bromley frowned. 'Might I ask why?'

'He has information on a case I'm working on.'

Bromley studied him for a moment and then nodded. 'OK. I'll have someone bring him up out of the hole.'

Fifteen minutes later, a guard led in a haggard-looking prisoner. He was filthy and stank of sweat. He eyed Ford and then returned his gaze to the gover-nor.

'Marshal Ford wants a word with you, Thomas.'

'Yes, sir.'

He turned to face Ford, who said, 'Before you answer what I'm about to ask you, I want you to think very carefully.'

'OK.'

'Do you know a feller named Bennett?'

'No.'

'Think about it.'

'I don't need to.'

Ford paused. 'Do you know why anyone wants you dead?'

Thomas frowned. 'What?'

The deputy marshal ignored him and turned to face Bromley. 'Warden, I have a transfer order in my pocket to take Thomas out of here for his own protection. His life is in danger.'

'Why haven't I heard of it?'

'It's only just come to light.'

'You'd best give it to me so I can read it, then.'

Ford reached into his pocket and took out the paper. He passed it to Bromley who perused it. He looked up and asked, 'Why didn't Bass have this all set out on the proper paper. It's just a hand-scrawled note. Anyone could have written it.'

'Like I said, last minute. If you need to get in touch with him, he's in Copper Bluffs. You'd have to send a rider, though, because they don't have telegraph. That's a four day round trip.'

Bromley studied him for a long moment and then nodded. 'OK. But I want you to sign release papers just in case this goes south, and they try to pin it on me.'

'Done.'

Three miles out from the prison, Ford pulled off the road into a large stand of pines, cut Thomas loose, and they dismounted.

'What's going on?' asked a wary Thomas.

'I've got more questions for you. I thought out here would be a better place and have less chance of you lying to me.'

'I don't know what you're talking about.'

'Just so you understand where we're at, a man's life depends on your answers. That, and I'm under instruction to kill you.'

Alarm flitted across Thomas' face. 'What? Why? I didn't do nothing.'

'Who wants you dead?'

'I don't know!'

'What did you do?'

'Nothing!'

'I'm going to say a few names and you tell me if you know them.'

'OK.'

'Ollie West. Milburn Allen. Chris Allen.'

With the mention of each name, Thomas grew a shade paler than before. He shook his head. 'I don't know them.'

'Liar!'

'No. I don't.'

Ford's Peacemaker came clear of leather. 'I'll give you to the count of three.'

He never even got to one before a shot rang out and Thomas grunted as the slug hammered home. He sank to his knees and rolled on to his side, a large red stain spreading across his shirtfront.

Ford whirled to face the threat. The gunfire rang out again, but this time the shooter missed. A furrow opened in the bark of a tree to Ford's right. A puff of gun-smoke gave away the bushwhacker's position. Ford snapped off a couple of shots in that direction and ducked behind a large pine.

More bullets peppered the trunk and sent bark chips flying.

Ford leaned out and fired two shots, paused, saw movement, and fired again. This time he was rewarded by a yelp of pain. He waited and when no more shots came, eased out from behind the tree.

Ford edged forward into the eerie silence that had descended across the stand of trees. When he reached the place where he figured the ambusher was, he was surprised to find a guard from the prison, down and dead.

Ford muttered, 'What the hell is going on?'

He went back to Thomas and found him still alive. Just. He knelt beside him and said, 'Tell me where I can find them.'

'Get me back to the prison doctor.'

Ford shook his head. 'You're dying. Whoever wanted you dead saw to that.'

'Milburn Allen.'

'Yes, Allen. Where can I find him?'

Thomas gave his head a weak shake. 'I don't know.'

'Something? Anything?'

Thomas said, 'Ollie West. Bender's Flats.' And then he died.

'Here's the wire you were expecting, Marshal,' said the Lost River telegrapher as he handed it over.

'Thanks,' Travers replied, and looked it over.

It read: *Names you asked about are on record. Trial three years ago. Murder of young woman. Maria Kemp. Thomas, witness. West, sheriff. Milburn Allen, judge. Chris Allen, suspect. Arresting officer, Bass Reeves.*

'Christ almighty,' Travers hissed. He knew of the case. But there was one name missing. The woman's

99

father, Oliver Kemp. He turned back to the telegrapher. 'I need you to send another wire for me.'

'Sure, what do you want to say?'

Two minutes later, the man tapped at his key until he was finished and then said, 'All sent.'

'How long until I get an answer?'

The telegrapher shrugged. 'Hard to say.'

'I'll wait.'

'Could be a while.'

'I'll still wait.'

And wait he did; for five hours, but when the reply came back, it was all worth it. It read:

Oliver Kemp lives Rock Flats, Montana.

'Son of a bitch,' Travers whispered.

CHAPTER 10

Bender's Flats was busy. Very busy. Bunting and streamers decorated the awnings on false-fronts. Hand-painted signs which said *Vote Ollie West for sheriff!* were scattered about. Along with others which said *Dan's your man! Vote for Dan Wells.* As he rode along the main street on the roan, Ford could sense the excitement in the air. Townsfolk stopped and glanced at the stranger, and then smiled.

When Ford found the law office, it was empty. He left the roan tied at the hitch-rail outside and set about searching for the sheriff. He hadn't gone far when he came across a small crowd outside the Gold Star Saloon, being addressed by the man himself.

'. . . and people, when you elect me sheriff again, I swear that I will do all I can to rid the town of the bad elements such as those on the outskirts of town.'

Ford saw the women in the group nod, while more than one of the men paled.

'Yes sir, Trixie and her girls will be gone by that evening.'

He continued to ramble on for several more minutes before finishing his promissory speech, and the crowd dissipated. He saw Ford and walked across to him. 'Howdy, stranger! Passing through?'

Ford studied the middle-aged man's face. He opened his jacket to show him the badge. 'Nope, I came to see you.'

West frowned. 'OK. Come on over to the office. We can talk there.'

Ford followed him back to the jail and climbed the steps to the boardwalk. They entered the office and the deputy marshal was surprised to find it relatively clean.

West walked across to a black pot-bellied stove and asked, 'Would you like a coffee?'

'Sure.'

West began to pour and said, 'So, what is it I can help you with?'

'Milburn Allen.'

West paused what he was doing, and then continued. 'Never heard the name before.'

'Thomas said different.'

'Elijah Thomas?'

'That's him.'

West finished pouring and turned to Ford with the steaming cup in his hand. Ford's right hand rested on the Peacemaker's butt, ready just in case.

West handed him the drink. 'What did he say I did? Roughed him up when I arrested him? He always said he'd get me for it. Maybe the warden. . . .'

'He's dead,' Ford stated.

'Really?'

'Yeah. But before he died he told me where you were. He said you'd know where to find Allen.'

'What did you say his name was?'

'Milburn Allen.'

West pretended to think long and hard, and then said, 'The only Allen I recall was a judge some years ago.'

'Do you know where he is?'

'Nope. Can't say as I do.'

West walked over to his battered desk and sat down. He looked about the heavily marked top as though he'd lost something, and then opened the first drawer.

Ford was caught by surprise when he looked up to see a Colt coming to bear on him. The hammer was thumbed back and aimed at him before he started his own draw.

The Peacemaker belched flame and the .45 calibre slug smashed into West's chest. The gun in the sheriff's fist discharged into the wall behind Ford.

The sheriff stiffened and slumped forwards, on to the desktop. Ford kept his gun trained on the inert form and stepped forward. He checked the body and found him dead.

'Christ,' he swore.

Outside, he heard footsteps on the boardwalk and the door burst open. Two men froze just inside the door when they saw Ford standing over the dead lawman with his Peacemaker still in his hand.

'It's all right, I'm a deputy marshal,' he said, trying to prevent them from drawing bad conclusions.

'What happened?' one of them asked.

'That's what I'd like to know,' Ford said.

'Your wire came back sooner than expected from Helena, Marshal,' the squint-eyed telegrapher said when Ford walked into the stuffy telegraph office.

Ford grunted and held out his hand.

The man passed it over and Ford read it. *Judge Milburn Allen, Daleyville Montana.*

He screwed up the piece of paper, a grim expression etched deep into his face. Hell, it just got better. First the prison, then the sheriff, and now, a damned judge.

'Your son is a very resourceful man, Marshal,' Kemp said, as he watched his prisoner eat the stew he'd brought down from the kitchen. 'He's getting through that list I had for him.'

'I told you, Kemp,' Bass growled, 'He'll be here for you. He's one of them young bucks who'll do whatever it takes to get their man. He might be a little unorthodox, but he's a damned good marshal.'

'Is that admiration I hear in the estranged father's tone.'

'Call it whatever you want. I'm just telling you how it is. He'll find you and he'll kill you. And I'll have a front-row seat to see it.'

'So you keep telling me. It's starting to get a little tedious, listening to your monotonous drivel.'

'We'll see. Enjoy life while you can, you stuck up son of a bitch.'

CHAPTER 11

The first thing Ford did when he hit the town of Daleyville was send word to Travers about what he'd found. The telegrapher asked him if he wanted to wait for a reply, but Ford told him that he would call back later. There was no saying how long it would take Travers to get the message anyway.

'Can you tell me where I might find Judge Allen at this time of day?' he asked the man behind the counter.

A wary look told him that he didn't want to say. 'Ahh . . .'

'What's the matter?'

'It's just that . . . just. . . .'

'Out with it.'

'You being a lawman should know what I mean.'

'No, I don't, damn it.'

'He's not quite legal, if you know what I mean?'

'You mean he's an outlaw?'

'Nooo, not exactly. He has different opinions on how the law should be enacted.'

'How do you mean?'

'Well, take his bodyguards for example.'

'He has bodyguards?'

The telegrapher nodded. 'Uh huh. There are three of them. Two were gunfighters who came before his bench. He found them guilty of manslaughter and gave them a choice. Work for him or go to prison for twenty years.'

'OK. What about the third?'

'That's even stranger. Have you heard of a man called Lacey Harper?'

Ford had. He was a killer the marshals had been after for years. 'I know of him.'

'Well, he's the third man. He came up before the judge and everyone expected him to hang. But, no. The judge had his men testify for him and the charges were dismissed.'

This was going to be tough. He needed answers from the judge, but with three dangerous men watching over him, it would not prove an easy task.

'What about his son? Do you know where he hangs his hat?'

The man shook his head.

'All right. Now, where can I find Judge Allen?'

'Are you sure?'

'Yeah.'

'He'll be at the Rolling Dice. It's where he has his office. He owns it, actually.'

Ford was about to leave when he had a thought. 'I want you to take down a message for me. And whatever you do, do not repeat a word of it.'

'Sure.'

The telegrapher took down the message and when he was finished, stared at Ford. 'Is that all?'

'Yeah. If something happens to me, you send it to the marshals.'

'OK.'

Ford left the telegraph office and led the roan along the street. Totally devoid of a plan, he figured to just throw dynamite and see what blew up. It was far from perfect, but so was life.

He found the saloon halfway along the street, and pushed in through the doors, finding the bar almost deserted.

As he crossed the floor, his boots clunked on the sawdust-covered boards. A round-faced barman approached Ford's position at the end of the rough-hewn counter.

'What can I get you, stranger?'

'I want to see the judge.'

'He ain't in at the moment,' the man lied.

'Do you know where I can find him?'

'Not as such.'

'Would you give him a message for me?'

'Sure.'

'Tell him, Thomas and West are dead. Tell him Thomas talked.'

The barkeep frowned. 'Is that it?'

'Yeah.'

'I'll tell him as soon as he gets back.'

'You do that.'

Ford turned away from the bar and walked out on

to the boardwalk. He held up a hand to shield his eyes against the glare of the bright sun, and stared in both directions for any sign of the judge. Across the street was a hotel, and beside it was a store where he could get the supplies he needed. He figured that would be a good place to go first. He stepped down into the street and waited until a flat-bed wagon passed him before he crossed. He climbed the steps on the other side and entered the store. Hopefully it wouldn't be too long before the judge came to find him.

The barkeep waited for Ford to leave, before going out to the back room of the saloon to find the judge, who was playing cards at a round table with his henchmen. He looked up and asked, 'What is it, George?'

'Just had a feller in here looking for you, Judge,' George said to him.

Allen was a large man with grey hair and a flabby face. He liked to wear black suits but often got his sizes mixed up, and more often than not they were ill-fitting.

The judge looked up from his hand. 'Who was he?'

'I don't know.'

'Well, what did he want?'

'He gave me a message for you. He said that Thomas and West were dead. And that Thomas talked.'

Allen froze. His face grew like stone. 'What else?'

109

'Nothing. That was it.'

'Where did he go?'

'He left. I presume he's still in town.'

Allen stared at his three hired guns. 'Find him, kill him. I'll pay you double for it.'

He shifted his gaze back to the barkeep. 'Go with them and make sure they know who he is.'

After they'd left, Allen reached across the polished tabletop and grasped a bottle of whiskey. He poured himself a drink with a trembling hand and tossed it back. His men would take care of it, he was certain of that.

'I thought that was your bad-tempered nag over there,' a voice said as Ford left the store. He turned to his right and saw a solidly built man in his mid-forties, a touch over six feet tall, standing on the boardwalk. About his waist he wore twin Colt Peacemakers, and atop his head was a low-crowned hat. He wore dark pants and a red shirt, and his face was weathered from years of travelling many trails.

Ford shook his head. 'Laramie Davis. It's been a while.'

Laramie nodded. 'It has. You still giving your old man grief?'

'Every chance I get.'

'I'd believe that. What are you doing in this dump?'

Across the street, four men emerged from the saloon. He saw the barkeep point in his direction and the three rough-looking men started over towards him.

'If I live through this, I'll tell you over a drink.'

He stepped down into the street, waiting for the men to draw nearer, then swept back his jacket to access his Colt. The trio of killers stopped no more than fifteen feet away.

'You fellers looking for me?'

'Uh huh,' Lacey Harper said with a nod.

There was movement beside Ford as Laramie stepped up to his shoulder. 'Got room for one more at this dance?'

'Ain't got nothing to do with you, stranger.'

'It has now.'

'You don't have to do this, Laramie,' Ford said.

'Thought it might be fun.'

Ford rolled his eyes and stared at Harper. 'I'll give you boys one chance. My name is Josh Ford. I'm a deputy marshal. I'm here to see the judge.'

'So?' said Lacey Harper.

Ford shrugged. 'All right. Call it.'

Hands flashed down and six-guns came up with deadly intent. They roared to life, and lead scythed through the air.

A slug from Ford's Peacemaker slammed into Harper's chest, rocking him violently. Another ripped into his throat, the ghastly wound spraying blood on to the street at his feet. He fell, twitching violently until he finally died, gasping for air.

Beside Ford, Laramie had his own guns out and working. The first of the two gunfighters on Allen's payroll died when a .45 calibre bullet punched into his chest, a second one through his skull.

The next gunman managed to get off a shot that flew wide of its mark before bullets from both Ford and Laramie punched his ticket in a violent fashion. He died with his boots drumming the earth and two bullets in his chest.

The deputy and the gunfighter stood there, staring at the dead men before them. Gun smoke still trickled from the barrels of their guns. Laramie asked, 'Are you going to tell me now?'

Ford's face took on a grim expression. 'Not yet. Come with me.'

As both men walked towards the saloon they dropped out the empty cartridges and replaced them with fresh loads. Ford stomped across the boardwalk with Laramie close behind. He crashed through the saloon doors and started towards the bar. He glared at the pale-faced barkeep and snarled, 'Where is he?'

The man pointed towards a rear door and the two men changed direction. The door to the back room stood no chance as Ford gave it a savage kick. It smashed back against the wall and the angry deputy entered the opulent space.

Behind the table, Allen grew wide-eyed when he saw the strangers before him.

'What do you want?' he blurted out.

'Answers,' Ford snapped. 'Right now.'

'I don't know what you mean.'

'Horseshit! Sure you do. Now tell me what you, your son, West and Thomas have in common.'

'Nothing.'

The Peacemaker came into Ford's hand and roared to life. The bullet took the judge in his left shoulder. He cried out in pain as blood began to appear from the wound.

'Let's start again,' Ford hissed. 'Or the next one goes in your head.'

CHAPTER 12

As Ford started to question Allen, Travers rode into Rock Flats. He figured he'd check in with the sheriff, as a courtesy more than anything. He found him at the jail, drinking coffee, perched behind a battered desk. Sheriff Hollister was a fat, slovenly man with unkempt hair.

'You're back, Marshal. What can I do for you this time around?' he asked Travers.

'I'm interested in one of your citizens,' Travers explained.

'Oh yes? Which one?'

'Oliver Kemp.'

'Mr Kemp? What did he do? Rob a train?' Hollister chuckled, and the rest of his body did too.

'Why do you laugh?'

'I'm sorry. It's just that if you knew Mr Kemp, you'd know there isn't a more gentlemanly man in the whole town.'

Travers nodded. 'Tell me about his daughter.'

Hollister's expression changed. He sat forward in

his seat and said, 'Maria? Yes, a terrible, terrible tragedy. She was such a lovely young lady.'

'What happened to her?'

'She was murdered by a young man three years ago. The marshals caught him, and the case went to trial.'

'You didn't catch him?'

Hollister shook his head. 'Maria was over in Westlake when it happened. The young man was put on trial there once they brought him in.'

'Do you know who it was caught up with him?'

'Yes, a marshal by the name of Reeves.'

'So, they hung him then? The young man?' Travers inquired.

Hollister snorted. 'Not likely. The trial was a farce from the start. The presiding judge was the young man's father.'

'How does that work? I would have thought he would have been excused?' Travers asked.

'Not likely when your name is Judge Millburn Allen. The sheriff found a witness who came forward and gave his son an alibi. That was it. The witness swore he was fifty miles away at the time of the murder. Case closed.'

'Was he?'

'Didn't matter.'

Travers nodded. 'I bet Kemp took that pretty hard, huh?'

'We all did. Like I said. Maria was lovely. Around here she was a ray of sunshine.'

'What happened to the young man after that?'

'Last I heard, he was working up in Helena.'

Travers stared at Hollister with a puzzled expression on his face.

'Oh, dear,' Hollister said, almost apologetically when he realized he'd slipped up. 'Did I say too much?'

When Travers looked, the sheriff had a six-gun in his hand, pointing toward him. 'What the hell is this?'

'Like I said, Marshal, Maria was a wonderful girl, and we all liked her. Now, what to do with you?'

'You won't get away with this.'

'Maybe, maybe not. Let's lock you up and we'll see.'

The cell was small, not much bigger than some of the prison ones he'd seen. The cot was iron-framed, and the mattress was lumpy and full of bugs. There was a window in the rear wall about six feet up.

Two men came into the office, both with badges on their shirts. One was solid, the other thin and willowy.

'What's going on?' they asked Hollister.

'The marshal here came nosing around asking questions. Had to put him up for a while. I was about to go up the hill and see the man.'

'Want us to come with you?'

Hollister nodded. 'Sure, why not. Get him out.'

'I don't think that was supposed to happen,' Laramie remarked.

'Damn it!' Ford cursed out loud. He hadn't even

got around to asking Allen about his son when his heart gave out.

'You want to tell me what all this was about now?'

Ford sighed. 'Someone's got Bass, and if I don't do as they say, they're going to kill him.'

'And Allen had something to do with it?'

'As far as I know he's a big part of it.' He went on to tell him about the prison, West, the sheriff, and everything else that had happened.

'And you have to kill all of them?'

'That's what the messenger said. So far, I've only done for West, and that was self-defence.'

'You did break that Thomas feller out of prison, though.'

'Yes, there is that.'

'How long before they figure out that it was a lie?'

Ford shrugged. 'They probably already know. But I can't worry about that. I have to find his son. I still have no idea who's behind all of this.'

'Last I heard, his boy was up in Helena,' Laramie said.

Ford stared at the gunfighter. 'How do you know?'

'Man in my profession hears things. You have to worry about how you're going to get to him.'

'Why?'

'He works for the governor.'

'Son of a bitch!'

'Exactly.'

Travers was escorted to the mansion on the hill by the lawman and his two deputies. Arriving at the opulent home, they were greeted by a well-dressed doorman who ushered them into the lavish study.

Kemp sat in a comfortable leather chair in the centre of the room, a glass of brandy in his hand. Beside him stood Harper, his bodyguard. Kemp studied Travers for a while before speaking.

'It would seem to me that Marshal Ford is as good an investigator as I predicted. I take it that you are working with him?'

Travers remained silent.

Kemp sighed. 'Never mind. I know that Thomas is dead. As is Sheriff West. I have also been informed that there have been inquiries concerning myself. By you, I assume, as you are here before me.'

Silence.

'Your silence is admirable but unnecessary. No one will be able to prove anything.'

Travers spoke, 'They won't have to prove anything. Once Ford finds you, he'll kill you. No second chance.'

Kemp laughed.

'You think it's funny?'

'I died the day they told me my daughter had been murdered.'

'And you're after everyone involved?'

'That's right. All of them.'

'What gives you the right. . . ?'

Kemp lunged to his feet and threw the glass to the floor at his feet. It shattered and sprayed shards and brandy across the cowhide mat.

'I have every damned right!' he screeched. 'They

118

were all responsible for the injustice that occurred after my daughter was murdered!'

'Even Bass?'

'Yes. Even him.'

'You're crazy.'

Kemp gathered himself. 'Sheriff Hollister, thank you for your loyalty in this matter. Mr Harper will take it from here.'

Hollister and his men left, and Harper crossed to Travers, a Colt in his right hand. 'Move.'

'Might help if I knew where to.'

Harper gave him a shove. 'Get going.'

'Couldn't have been that stubborn son of mine, could it?' Bass growled.

'Good to see you too,' Travers said. 'Next time, I'll come shooting.'

'Might be best.'

'How wonderful,' Kemp said with heavy sarcasm. 'Make the most of it. It won't last.'

'What?' Travers asked, a frown on his face.

Kemp nodded to Harper and the bodyguard raised his gun and shot the marshal in the head.

'You son of a bitch!' Bass roared as he came off the floor. He lunged at Harper and caught the man by surprise. Harper had strayed within the radius of the reach of the chain and, although Bass was weakened by his time in captivity, he hit him hard. Harper staggered as the marshal grappled for his gun. A clawed hand wrapped around it and Harper cursed as he tried to wrench the weapon free.

But Bass wasn't about to let it go without a fight. Harper's face drew within range and the marshal snapped his head forward. The blow missed its intended target of the bridge of Harper's nose, but caught him flush on the forehead.

Instead of bringing the bodyguard to his knees, it rattled the weakened marshal to his core. His legs buckled and his grip on the Colt loosened.

Harper felt triumphant through his anger as he ripped the weapon free and aimed it at Bass' head.

'Hold it!'

Harper held his fire while Bass stood before him, growling a deep, guttural noise. The marshal spoke in a low voice, 'I'm going to kill you, you bastard.'

Harper smiled at him. 'We'll see.'

CHAPTER 13

'Just keep your hand away from your gun, Marshal Ford,' the steady voice cautioned him. 'I don't want to have to shoot you.'

Ford kept his hands out from his side and turned slowly from the counter of the store.

'Just take it easy, Lem,' he said. 'I ain't going to pull on you.'

Lem Bates was sheriff of Chester, a small town some twenty miles south of Helena. Ford and Laramie had stopped off to get some supplies to tide them over the rest of the way.

Laramie was off to the side and dropped his hand to his right-side six-gun.

'Wait, Laramie,' Ford told the gunfighter. 'Let's see if we can talk it through.'

The deputy turned his attention to Lem. 'What's going on, Lem?'

'Word came that if you were sighted, you was to be arrested,' the sheriff explained.

'Why?'

'Story is you busted a feller out of the pen. Killed

him and a guard who came after you.'

'Not true.'

'Not what they say. The wire's singing for anyone who comes across you to lock you up for murder.'

'Come on, Lem, you know me.'

'I do, but it don't make any difference.'

'Call it, Josh,' Laramie said from the side.

'Wait.'

Laramie shrugged.

'Where am I to be sent?' Ford asked.

'I guess I'll find that out when I wire them that want you.'

Ford nodded. The last thing he wanted was to have a confrontation with Lem. After all, he was just doing his job. 'All right, I'll come peaceable.'

Relief flooded the sheriff's face. 'Thanks, Josh.'

'They're going to send some marshals for you,' Lem told Ford. 'They should be here tomorrow.'

'Did they say who?'

'Feller called Willis.'

'Roy Willis?'

'That's him. You ain't the only one they'll be here to get though.'

Ford looked at the cell beside him. 'Who is he?'

'Brick Carlisle.'

Ford nodded. He'd heard of Carlisle. Mean killer from Kansas. Wanted for murdering a bunch of people. 'Going for a rope date?'

'Sure is.'

'Go to hell,' the man snapped.

'I guess you'll be there before me,' Ford pointed out.

Carlisle muttered something under his breath that Ford ignored. Then the outlaw said, 'I won't be here long enough anyway.'

'We'll see,' said Lem.

'Yeah, we will.'

'What do you want me to do, Josh?' Laramie asked, and his question put the sheriff on edge.

'We wait for Willis and the others to get here tomorrow. In the meantime, do you think you can stay out of trouble?'

Laramie snorted. 'The name's Davis, not Ford.'

'Yeah, I know.'

Honest Jim Manson halted his horse on the edge of Chester just as the orange fingers of the sun's last rays reached out across the western sky. Behind him were five others, all here to break their boss out of jail.

'Are we just going to ride in there and bust him out, Jim?' an ugly, scar-faced man named Barrett asked.

'That's the plan. There's only one lawdog in the place. Should be easy enough.'

'How about we rob the bank while we're there?' asked a thin-faced outlaw.

Manson considered it and then nodded. 'All right. Three of you get Brick out and the rest of us will do just that.'

'Let's go then,' Barrett said enthusiastically.

'No, wait until morning when the bank is open. Let's get off the road and find a place to camp. No fire, we don't want anyone knowing we're here.'

CHAPTER 14

Seven men. Seven strangers. Seven of them. They rode into Chester and drew attention straightaway. Why wouldn't they? They were all rough-looking and had an aura of meanness about them.

Manson rode at the head of them, followed by Barrett. And then came Burke, Wills, Trantor, Coyle and Ingram. With a single hand motion, Barrett, Burke and Trantor split off and rode towards the jail. The rest made for the bank.

On the boardwalk outside the jail, Lem saw them coming. He knew they were trouble, long before they divided their forces.

His mind whirred and he wished he had a deputy to back his play. But alas, the town council had not deemed it necessary to give him one, even though the town was growing steadily.

Lem muttered a curse under his breath and retreated inside.

'Of all the damned days,' he growled as he walked across the room to the gun rack on the wall. 'As if I don't have enough troubles.'

Ford came off the bunk in the cell. 'What's up, Lem?'

'Strangers in town,' he said as he checked over the Winchester he'd taken down. 'Seven of them. Three are coming this way and the rest are out front of the bank. My guess is that they're Carlisle's bunch.'

'I told you,' he guffawed.

'Shut up.'

'Let me out, Lem. I can help you,' Ford urged him.

'I can't do that, you're my prisoner.'

Ford cursed under his breath. 'Damn it, Lem, you don't stand a chance on your own. Let me out. Think of Mary.'

Mary was Lem's pregnant wife.

He knew Ford was right, and every fibre of his being told him that it wasn't a good idea, but: 'You promise you won't try to run?'

'No, I won't.'

'All right,' the sheriff said and scooped the keys from his desk.

'Looks like you're both gonna die before this is over,' Carlisle stated.

Keys rattled in the lock and the door swung open. Ford stepped through and Lem said, 'Your gun is in the cupboard against the wall.'

Ford found the Peacemaker and strapped it on. He checked the loads and rammed it back into the holster.

'How do you want to play this, Lem?' he asked.

'I was hoping you'd tell me.'

'It's your town.'

'How about we just go out there and take them head on?'

'Wouldn't have it any other way.'

Laramie was looking out the window of his hotel room when he saw them ride in. Like Lem, he knew they were trouble. When he saw them split up, he walked across to his bed and unhooked the double gun belt from over the post. He strapped it on and headed for the door.

Out in the hall, he saw a young lady walking towards the stairs. He called after her, 'Are you going out, miss?'

She halted and gave him a questioning look. 'Why, yes, I am.'

'I'd leave that thought for a moment. Things are apt to get a little wild downstairs shortly.'

'Rain?' she asked.

Laramie shook his head. 'Shooting.'

'Oh,' she said and then realization settled in: 'Oohhh!'

'Yes, ma'am, that's about right.'

The gunfighter took the stairs two at a time until he hit the floor in the foyer. He walked to the front doors and out on to the boardwalk.

He stared in the direction the men had gone. Three were at the jail and the other four were hauling rein outside the bank. This was not good.

Laramie thought for a moment and then nodded.

127

He drew both Peacemakers and stepped out on to the street. He was just in time to see Ford and Lem come out of the jail, guns blazing.

Ford was first through the door, his Colt level with his waist. The three outlaws froze when they saw him.

The six-gun roared, and Barrett grunted as the slug hit him in the middle. A puff of dust from his clothing was the tell-tale sign of the bullet strike. Ford thumbed back the hammer and shot him again. This time the lead burned deep into his chest and Barrett lurched into the man behind him.

Trantor tried to push the mortally wounded man away from him and bring his six-gun into play against the threat.

Beside Ford, Lem fired his own six-gun, a .45 calibre Schofield. The bullet struck Burke in the chest and the outlaw cried out. Still erect, he was able to get off a couple of shots. One burned through the air close to the sheriff and hammered into the jail-house wall behind him. The second tore through the fabric and flesh of the lawman's gun arm.

Lem's hand went numb and his fingers opened, dropping the Schofield to the boardwalk. 'I'm hit!' he exclaimed.

Ford cursed and fired two shots at Tranter as he cleared himself of Barrett. Both slugs punched into the outlaw's chest who was dead before he hit the hard-packed gravel beside Barrett. The deputy marshal then shifted his aim to the third outlaw.

However, Burke was now under the full effect of

the two bullets Lem had put in him, and was sinking to his knees. Ford made sure he was done, with a bullet to his head.

'Lem, are you OK?'

'Hit in the shoulder,' he said through gritted teeth. 'Damn it. There's still four more of them.'

Ford dropped out the spent cartridges from the Colt and started to replace them with fresh rounds. He was about done when more gunfire erupted. This time it was further along the street. He rammed in the last bullet and closed the loading gate. Then he stepped out on to the street and looked along to where the gunfire raged. Then he saw Laramie go down and a feeling of dread descended over him.

Once he hit the street, Laramie's weapons worked with a well-oiled ease. He walked steadily towards the outlaws and opened fire.

The outlaws had been facing the other way, their guns out as they watched the battle at the jail further along the dusty street. The gunfighter fired his first shot and Coyle dropped like a stone. The other three whirled about and Laramie's second shot flew wide of its mark.

Lead stormed through the air as the outlaws fired with wild abandon. Laramie felt the hot rush of air near his face as the bullets almost kissed his skin. He fired again, and Ingram lurched to the left with a bullet in his arm.

A barrage of slugs came at the gunfighter, and he was just wondering how they were missing him when he felt a hammer blow radiate through his right leg. It went numb, and refused to hold Laramie's weight. He fell to the hard-packed earth of the street, vulnerable and a sitting target.

With pain shooting up his leg, the gunfighter rolled on to his stomach to find another target. The remaining three were still firing at him, causing small geysers of earth to erupt around him. It was only a matter of time before one killed him.

A grim smile split Ford's lips when he saw his friend move. At least he was still alive. For the moment. But not for long if he didn't do something.

Ford let the hammer fall on a fresh round and Wills shot forwards as the bullet burned deep between his shoulder blades.

Manton whirled and saw Ford coming towards him. He raised his six-gun and fired at the deputy marshal. A puff of dirt erupted at Ford's feet. The outlaw fired again, and this time Ford felt it tug at the material of his shirt.

Ford fired back and missed, but the next shot found flesh and Manton went up on his toes before Ford sighted and fired again. Manton fell backwards to the unforgiving earth and didn't move.

Now, the only outlaw left was the wounded Ingram who suddenly had second thoughts about dying and dropped his weapon, throwing his hands in the air.

'Don't shoot!'

Ford kept him covered and walked forwards. In the background, he saw Laramie start to climb to his feet. 'You all right?' he called to the gunfighter.

Laramie began a laboured limp towards them. 'Bastard shot the heel off my boot. Hurt like hell.'

'Thought they'd got you for a moment.'

Footsteps sounded beside him, and Ford turned his head. Lem stood there, his arm cradled against the pain. 'Are you OK?'

The sheriff grimaced. 'I'll live. How about you two?'

Laramie limped over to them and said, 'Never felt better.'

CHAPTER 15

'Riders coming in,' Laramie said through the open front door to the jail.

Ford put down his cup of coffee on the desk and walked outside to stand near the gunfighter. He looked along the street and saw them: four riders on tired-looking horses. They were led by a thin-faced man with slim hips and shoulders. His name was Roy Willis.

The men drew up to the hitch rail outside the jail and Willis said, 'Ain't you on the wrong side of the cell door?'

Ford shrugged. 'Had a slight problem.'

'Laramie,' Willis greeted the gunfighter with a nod.

'Roy.'

Willis and the other marshals climbed down. 'Want to tell me what's going on?'

'Brick Carlisle's gang rode in. Thought they could cut him loose and rob the bank at the same time. They figured wrong. We helped Lem out.'

Willis took Ford's hand and the two men shook.

'It's good to see you, Josh. Mind you, I wish it was under better circumstances.'

'Me too, Roy.'

'How about we go inside and have a chat?'

Ford nodded. 'Sure. How about the saloon?'

'You're still a prisoner, you know?'

'Condemned man has to have a last drink.'

Willis gave him a wry smile. 'That's a meal, but what the hell. Coming, Laramie?'

'Since you're buying, I ain't going to knock it back.'

Willis shook his head. 'I knew there was a catch to it somewhere.'

The three men sat around a battered table, sharing a bottle of watered-down liquid that tasted as though some cowhand had washed his socks in it. The other marshals were at another table not far away.

Willis stared at Ford and said, 'Right, talk to me.'

Ford sighed. 'So, you know Bass has disappeared, right?'

'Bit hard not to since I've been put in charge. Come on, Josh, stop wasting time.'

'Ben Travers and I are working together to track him down. We met up in Bender's Gulch and while we was there, I received a note about Scar Ferguson. It said if I didn't go and brace him, Bass would be killed. After that was done, a feller appeared at our camp and had on him a paper with a list of names.'

'I know about the names,' Willis said. 'Travers messaged us, and we did some digging. Apparently they

133

are all connected through a case and Bass was the arresting officer. Travers went back over to Rock Flats to follow a lead. Tell me about the prison.'

'I forged transfer papers and got Thomas out. The feller who delivered the list of names said they were all to be killed.'

A long breath escaped Willis' lips. 'Damn it, Josh.'

'It ain't what you think. One of the guards followed us and snuck up after dark and shot him. I killed the guard. I figure the guard had a purpose to watch over Thomas to make sure he wouldn't talk. But he gave me the names of Milburn Allen and West. West was the only one he knew the location of.'

'And you went and killed him.'

Ford shook his head. 'Nope. Well, yes.'

'Christ,' Willis swore. 'I might as well turn my badge in now. No wonder your old man grumbled so much.'

'West tried to shoot me in his office. I had no choice. And then there's Milburn.'

Ford saw the expression of dread cast a shadow over Willis' face. Laramie sat forward and said, 'In our defence, his heart gave out before we could question him too much.'

Willis rolled his eyes. 'This just gets better. You were there?'

'I was.'

'For a man who's sworn to uphold the law and was trying not to kill anyone, you sure failed in that respect.'

'You don't know the best part yet,' Ford pointed out.

Willis' voice dripped with sarcasm. 'Do tell.'

'Milburn's son works for the governor. Apart from Bass, he's the only one left who knows what the hell is going on.'

'Not quite true,' Willis said. 'After Travers sent word asking about them, like I said, I looked into it myself. Apparently the young man in question was acquitted at trial for the murder of a young lady named Maria Kemp. It turns out her father lives in Rock Flats, which is where Bass was when he went missing.'

'You think that is a coincidence?' Ford asked.

'Be a mighty big one if it was,' Willis said.

Ford started to rise from the chair. 'Well, then that's where I'm going.'

'You seem to forget, I have a prior claim, Josh.'

He sat back down. 'You know Bass could be there, Roy.'

'He could, but if he was, do you think we might have heard by now from Ben?'

'You haven't heard from him?'

'Nope. Not since the last inquiry about Allen.'

Ford got back to his feet. 'Come on, Laramie, are you in?'

'Until the end.'

'Wait!' Willis called after them. His voice sounded tired. 'I'm coming too. Can't have my prisoner running around everywhere unsupervised.'

Willis stood and turned to the other marshals. 'Head back to Helena. See what you can find out about Milburn Allen's son. We'll be a few days.'

They left the saloon and hurried along to the livery to get their horses ready. By the time they rode out of town, the sun was almost down.

Oliver Kemp sat in front of his fireplace with a tumbler of brandy. He stared at the orange and blue flames that licked at the fresh logs. A knock sounded at the study door and he turned his head to look at it.

The knock sounded again.

Kemp sighed. 'Yes?'

The door opened, and Harper entered. In his hand was a piece of paper. 'News, Mr Kemp.'

The bodyguard crossed the floor and gave Kemp the note, who opened it and read. After a couple of minutes, he stared at Harper. 'It would seem that our Marshal Ford is quite capable. Milburn Allen can be scratched from our list.'

'That just leaves Chris Allen, sir.'

Kemp's face darkened. 'I've told you before, Harper, I'll not have his name spoken in this house.'

'Sorry, sir.'

'It won't be long and he'll be here. A week maybe, after he takes care of the final matter.'

'Providing he does what he's supposed to do and works out where we are?'

Kemp stared into the flames. 'I'm quite sure that by the time he's finished, he'll know where to come.'

'I hope so, sir.'

'Have Hollister start work on the gallows tomorrow. With two ropes. We'll hang them side by side.'

'I'll see to it, Mr Kemp.'

'Good. That'll be all.'

'Yes, sir.'

Harper left the room and it grew quiet. Every now and then a pop and crackle from the fire could be heard. Kemp stared down at the picture on his lap. 'Soon, my dear Maria, it will all be over soon.'

CHAPTER 16

It wasn't long after noon two days later when the three riders arrived at Rock Flats.

'How do you want to play this, Josh?' Willis asked.

'You're the boss, Roy,' Ford said. 'What do *you* want to do?'

'I was thinking if Laramie rides in with us, it'll draw too much attention. Especially with that bronc he's riding.'

Laramie's horse snorted. Bo was a chocolate-coloured appaloosa. A big, one-man horse which had been given to him by a Cheyenne warrior some time back.

'Maybe he can ride in alone and find himself a room. You and I will ride in together and get you locked away in the jail. That way if they want you, they'll have to come and get you.'

Ford couldn't believe what he was hearing. 'Like a chicken ripe for the plucking. No thanks.'

'You'll be fine. You don't think I'd leave you

138

hanging, do you? Between me and Laramie, we'll keep an eye out.'

'I don't like it.'

'You don't have to like it, just do it.'

They drew up in the centre of the road and Ford reached down and unbuckled the gun belt. He tossed it across to Willis. The marshal caught it and placed it in his saddle-bag.

Laramie said, 'I guess I'll see you gents later on.'

'I'll meet you in the saloon after dark. We can have a meal and a drink.'

Ford grumbled something under his breath.

'What was that?' Willis asked.

'I said don't choke.'

They chuckled, and Ford grumbled once more.

'Hey, Buck. Riders coming in. That makes three this afternoon,' the deputy called from outside on the boardwalk.

Hollister dragged his backside from the off-kilter timber chair and walked slowly across to the door. He left the jail and stood beside his deputy. They watched the riders draw closer and before long they were able to recognize the badge on Willis' coat.

'He's a marshal.'

'Another one,' the deputy said and dropped his hand to his six-gun.

'Easy,' Hollister cautioned. 'Let's just see what it's all about. Might be he just wants to use the cell for the night.'

Willis and Ford eased their horses to a halt at the

hitch rail. Willis greeted them and said, 'You wouldn't have a cell I could borrow for the night would you, sheriff?'

Hollister ran a wary eye over them and nodded, 'Sure. I think we can do that, Marshal. . . ?'

'Roy Willis.'

'Buck Hollister. Who's our friend here?'

Willis shook his head. 'I'm ashamed to say this feller is one of our own. Wanted for the murder of two people. His name is Josh Ford.'

Hollister froze. Surprise came to his face and he said, 'One of your own, you say?'

'Yeah. We'll continue to Helena tomorrow and he'll stand trial there.'

'Climb down,' Hollister said. 'I'll show you where the cells are, and you can lock him in.'

The manacles worn by Ford rattled as he climbed down. Both horses were tied to the hitch rail and Willis and Ford went inside. Behind them, Hollister gave his deputy a knowing look and he nodded his understanding. He turned and hurried along the boardwalk.

Once inside, Willis took the manacles off Ford's wrists and mouthed, 'OK?'

Ford nodded.

Once he was locked away, Willis turned to Hollister. 'I'll be back around dark to check on him.'

'Sure, he'll be right here. It ain't like he'll be going anywhere.'

'If he does, it's your head.'

*

Kemp sat on his verandah and looked out over the town before him. He noted the urgency of the approaching man and frowned. 'Harper?'

'Yes, sir?' the bodyguard called from inside.

'We have a visitor.'

The screen door squeaked as it opened and Harper stepped outside. He stared down the hill and said, 'One of the sheriff's deputies.'

'Yes.'

The man stopped at the bottom of the steps. He puffed and blew while he tried to gather himself. Once he'd done so, he looked up and said, 'He's here.'

'Who?' Kemp snapped with impatience.

'The marshal, Ford. He's in the jail.'

Kemp sat up straight. 'Keep going.'

'He was brought in by another marshal. Has him under arrest for murder. He's keeping him in the jail overnight and leaving tomorrow.'

'Just the one marshal?' Kemp asked.

'Yes, sir. There was another feller come into town earlier but he's just a drifter by the looks of him.'

Harper said, 'I'll go get him.'

Kemp wasn't sure. They'd already suffered the interference of one marshal, now another just happens along with the man they require. And then there was the stranger.

He said, 'Tell Hollister to bring them all to me. Get enough men and bring all three here. I won't have everything undone now we're so close.'

'Are you sure, Mr Kemp?' Harper asked.

'Yes. Do it now. We'll hang Reeves and his son tomorrow.'

The deputy nodded. 'Sure, Mr Kemp. We can finish the gallows today.'

'Good, see to it.'

The two men watched the deputy hurry down the hill. Kemp said, 'This is it, Mr Harper. The moment we've waited for.'

'Get up!' the man standing before Willis said. 'Now.'

The marshal stared at the guns pointed at him and then at the men holding them. He hesitated and then rose to his feet.

'What is this?'

'You're to come with us,' the deputy snapped.

'You do realize that I'm a deputy marshal, right?'

A man moved around behind Willis and relieved him of his six-gun.

'Let's go.'

'You won't get away with this.'

'The other deputy said something similar.'

'Ford?'

'No, the other one.'

'Travers? Where is he?'

'Boothill.'

Willis felt anger rise from deep within. He stared at the deputy. 'What's your name?'

The man frowned. 'Brown.'

'I'm going to kill you, Brown.'

'Move.'

*

The cell door swung open and Ford stared at the gun in Hollister's hand. 'Out.'

'So, you're in it too, huh?'

Hollister stepped aside as the deputy marshal moved forward through the door. 'Yeah, I am.'

'What about your deputies?'

'You'd be surprised.'

'Where are we going?'

'To see Mr Kemp. You and your old man have a date with the hangman tomorrow.'

'Bass is still alive?'

Hollister gave him a mirthless smile. 'Sure he is. Not like that other marshal, Travers. We kinda had to do away with him.'

Ford ground his teeth together. A curse formed on his lips.

'Come on,' Hollister said. 'We can't keep Mr Kemp waiting. This has been a long time coming.'

Ford nodded. 'You're right. Let's not keep the son of a bitch waiting for his death any longer.'

From up in his cramped single room, Laramie watched the street below. He'd seen the deputy hurry along the street and up the hill towards the double-storey mansion atop it. Then he watched the man come back down and walk into the jail.

Soon after, he'd reappeared and walked along to the saloon. He was in there for around five minutes before he came out with four other men. They'd headed for the hotel.

Then two other things happened. Three more

men emerged from the saloon with Willis, and across the street at the jail, the sheriff and his other deputy emerged with Ford.

A grim expression appeared on Laramie's face. 'It didn't take long.'

Then he realized what the other men were doing, the five he'd observed coming towards the hotel: they were coming for him.

Time to go.

He remembered seeing a door at the end of the hallway. Hopefully a way out. He scooped up the Winchester from his bed and moved quickly towards the door. When he emerged from his room, the gun-fighter could already hear their approach as boots clumped up the stairs.

Laramie hurried along to the door and tried it. It swung clear of the jamb and he'd been right: it opened out on to a landing with stairs that led down into the alley beside the hotel.

When the door snicked shut behind him, the deputy and his makeshift posse had just started to make their way along the hallway.

They burst into the room but found it empty. One of the men said, 'He was supposed to be here.'

'Yeah,' said the deputy. 'That means he saw us coming.'

CHAPTER 17

Laramie descended the steps two at a time and walked along the alley towards the rear of the building. The back street was almost deserted. He turned in the direction of the mansion on the hill and jogged along until he figured he was ahead of the two escorts. Then he found an alley and headed back to the main street. Before he stepped out into the advancing crowd's path, he drew his right-side Colt and thumbed the hammer back on the Winchester.

'That's far enough!' Laramie's voice brought them to a halt. 'Time for you gents to make a choice. Make the right one and you might just see the sun go down.'

Hollister stepped forward. 'You are interfering with official law business, friend. Step aside.'

'Two things, *friend*! First thing first. I ain't your friend. Second, if you don't turn them loose, I'm going to put a .45 slug in your fat guts. Make your decision.'

'Five against one. I like them odds.'

Ford shook his head. 'Hell, just shoot the tub of lard, Laramie.'

The sheriff paled. 'You're Laramie Davis?'

'Surprise!' Laramie said and squeezed the trigger of the Colt.

There was a hollow thunk as the slug buried deep into the rolls of the sheriff's middle, driving the air from his lungs.

'Josh!' Laramie called out, and threw the Winchester in his direction. The deputy marshal caught it and swung it around. He fired the weapon at the man nearest him and the bullet hammered into his chest.

Two men down.

Laramie fired at Hollister's deputy, who cried out. The man had been moving and was only wounded in the left arm. Chaos started to reign, and the good citizens of Rock Flats began to scatter and find cover.

Roy Willis dropped beside the man Ford had killed, and with swift movements, unbuckled the gun belt. He drew the sidearm and came erect, sighted on the first fleeing form he could see, and let the hammer on the six-gun drop.

The man cried out and was thrust forward as though shoved by an invisible hand. He sprawled in the dust of the street and didn't move.

Willis whirled around, 'Josh, go find Bass.'

Ford shot another of the escort men and called across, 'You be all right?'

'Laramie and I got this.'

'What about them?'

146

Willis saw the five men advancing on them from down the street, the deputy called Brown at their head.

'Oh, yeah. I'm sure.'

As Ford raced along the street towards the mansion on the hill, Laramie fired three shots at the wounded deputy, who sought shelter behind a water trough. The first two bullets smacked into the thick timber, the third was lucky enough to strike the man as he came up to fire his gun.

He flailed back with a bullet in his throat, blood spraying out of the ghastly wound. A storm of lead cracked close to the gunfighter and he saw the five men who had joined the affray. He moved to his right and up on to the boardwalk. He found shelter in a recessed doorway and went to fire again.

The hammer fell on an empty chamber and the gunfighter cursed. Laramie dropped the gun into its holster and drew the left one. With his back to the rough surface of the door, he edged out cautiously and snapped off two more shots.

By now, Roy Willis had found cover behind a water barrel at the mouth of an alley on the far side of the street. A couple of slugs whacked into the timber before him and splinters sliced through the air.

As he rose from behind his refuge, he saw a clear target and fired two shots at the chosen man, watching him fall as the wounded leg gave out. It was then that he saw Deputy Brown disappear along an alley near the saddlery, trying to circle around and get behind him and Laramie.

'Not today, you son of a bitch,' Willis growled, and came to his feet. He fired a couple more shots and ducked down the alley nearest him.

He ran past a set of steps and an open window, and then as he left the alley, Brown was there before him. Both were surprised at their proximity to each other, and their guns blazed wildly.

In their desperate haste, shots flew wide as they tried to kill one another. A slug scored the flesh of Willis' side and brought forth a curse from the lawman. He fired again at Brown and heard the man grunt as the bullet tore through the gut just above the belt buckle. Brown sank to his knees and dropped his six-gun.

Brown stared up at Willis with pain etched on his face. The deputy marshal raised his gun and said, 'I told you I'd kill you, you son of a bitch.' Then he squeezed the trigger.

Meanwhile, back around the front, Laramie had depleted his loads and thumbed in fresh ones before closing the loading gate. He peered around the corner of the recess and saw at least four bodies on the street. A man started a dash across the street and the gunfighter fired at him but missed.

A storm of lead came his way, gouging timber splinters from the framework and scything them through the air. Another shattered the large front window.

He ducked back and waited for the firing to die down. Once it had abated some, he eased forwards once more and this time saw two men coming towards him. With practised skill, he fired at them. One dived to the street, while the other screamed and clutched at his arm. He ran off to the side and found an alley to duck into. The sound of distant gunfire sounded which stopped him in his tracks, and he staggered and fell dead on the ground.

Willis emerged from the alley and started firing at an unseen target. Suddenly the man in the street cried out, 'Don't shoot! I've had enough!'

He climbed to his feet and raised his hands. Soon more men appeared, even more than had started out. And just like that, the battle on the main street was over.

With the gunfire still sounding behind him, Ford jogged up the hill towards the house. Maybe if he'd had more time he might have stopped to admire its magnificence. But he didn't. Instead, he walked through the gate and up on to the veranda.

Ford tried the door and it swung open a fraction. On the other side, a gun opened fire and small needle-like slivers of wood sprayed outward as the bullets smashed through it.

The deputy marshal felt a sting on his right cheek as a splinter sliced at the flesh. Blood flowed freely and Ford cursed when more bullets crashed through the door. As soon as the staccato drum stopped, he kicked the door open and fired the Winchester. Then he levered and fired again.

The man on the other side of the door in the entrance hall, shuddered as the two bullets struck home. The dark suit he wore showed twin holes where the slugs had torn through it and his life-giving blood flowed freely.

Ford levered a round into the breech of the Winchester once more and fired again. Tennison lurched back and slumped to the floor, his rifle clattering when it landed beside him.

The deputy marshal edged into the cavernous hall and listened. The silence within was almost deafening. Ford's heart beat a loud drum in his ears. Then, 'Down here! Down. . . .'

Ford moved towards an open doorway. When he reached it he saw the stairs that led down into the cellar. He took a couple of tentative steps down, one of the treads creaking under his weight. In the silence it was loud enough to make the deputy marshal wince.

Suddenly, at the bottom of the stairs, a man with a six-gun appeared. He fired three rapid shots and Ford felt one of them rake his ribs. The lawman bit back a pained curse and fired a shot at the man who reeled away out of sight.

Ford kept his forward motion down the steps until he reached the bottom. The room was lit by a large lantern which cast a shadow-dappled orange glow throughout. The wounded man squirmed on the cold, hard floor.

Against the far wall, he could see two figures. One was seated and appeared to be chained. The other, a well-dressed man, held a gun to the figure's head.

With the Winchester canted across his body, Ford

said, 'You OK, Bass?'

Bass raised his head. His face was covered in grime and a full beard, his eyes weary, hair a dirt-ridden mess. 'Knew I could rely on you, boy. Now kill this son of a bitch and let's get out of here.'

'Just hold it, marshal,' Kemp snapped. 'In case you haven't noticed, I have the upper hand here.'

'Shoot him!' Bass hissed.

Ford ignored him. 'Tell me, Kemp. I can understand the others, but why Bass? He had nothing to do with the death of your daughter.'

'He was involved. He let them get away with it. He knew that the witness was false and did nothing.'

Bass' eyes blazed. 'I could do nothing, damn it. Yes, I knew. But by the time I got there for the trial, it was over and my hands were tied.'

Ford nodded. 'There you go.'

'He could have done something. Which makes him responsible. And for that, he should die like the rest of them.'

Ford sensed rather than saw Kemp's finger tighten on the trigger. He swung the Winchester around and squeezed the trigger. The man lurched under the impact of the slug and Bass shrank back as he waited for the slug to burn into his brain.

Kemp fell to his knees, the six-gun slipping from his grasp. Ford heard a single word escape his lips as he fell to his side and died: 'Maria!'

'Get me outta these damned chains, boy,' Bass growled. From behind the deputy, Harper moaned. 'Come on, I'm going to kill his ass. He shot Ben

151

Travers right here in this room.'

'Let it go, Bass, there's been enough killing here today.'

'The hell there has,' Bass hissed. 'You ain't been chained up down here for months.'

Ford turned away from his father and started to walk towards the steps.

'Where the hell are you going?'

'There's still one person left on the list.'

'Get me outta the chains, Josh. Now!'

He kept walking.

'Josh!'

Kept walking.

'*Josh*!'

He passed Willis on the steps. 'Let him loose, will you?'

Ford finished climbing the steps and stared around the entry hall. For the first time he saw it for what it was. An empty shell of grandeur. It was obvious that all the money in the world couldn't take Kemp's pain away.

Laramie entered through the front door. 'You OK?'

He nodded.

'What about your old man?'

'He's still breathing fire, as always.'

Laramie smiled.

Behind him, Ford could hear the angry footsteps as Bass stomped up the stairs. 'Where the hell is that boy?'

When he came out, he was surprised to see

Laramie standing there. 'You!'

'Howdy, Bass.'

'Are you mixed up in this mess, too?'

Laramie nodded. 'You might say that I'm along for the ride. Thought Josh might need a hand seeing as he's wanted for murder and prison break.'

Bass glared at his son, eyes sparked. 'What?'

'It ain't what you think. Besides, it was all in the name of saving your sorry ass.'

'That's why you left me chained up down there.'

Ford shook his head. 'It's got me beat why they didn't just let you go of their own free will. I bet if they had their time over again they'd do just that.'

'What are you saying?'

'Nothing, Bass. Nothing at all.'

CHAPTER 18

A week later, four riders rode into Helena on a final mission. Bass, after a bath, fresh clothes, a shave and haircut, looked to be back to his old self. Even his temperament seemed to have returned.

'I can't believe you were going to leave me chained there,' he growled for the hundredth time. 'Your own flesh and blood.'

'Maybe I should've let him shoot first,' Ford commented.

'You'd like that, wouldn't you? I think maybe I should send you back to Texas. Or better still, a stint in the Nevada desert. That might take some starch outta your pants.'

'The only starch I got in my pants, old man, was put there by you.'

Willis chuckled. 'He's right there, Bass.'

'I take it that you would like to join him, Roy?'

'The apple didn't fall far from the tree, Bass,' Laramie said.

The marshal glared at the gunfighter. 'How would

you like a job once this is over?'

'Is that a threat, Bass?'

'No, damn it. I thought you might like to replace my *son*!'

'I'll think about it.'

Ford shook his head. 'I don't believe it. Laramie Davis thinking about putting the badge back on.'

Bass said, 'There are a few towns still need cleaning up. Walt Grimes told me of a place down in Texas he might need a hand with. It's called Dent, I think.'

'Oh, Christ,' Ford mumbled.

'What was that?'

'Never mind.'

Bass turned towards Laramie. 'You're sure he works for the governor?'

'Last I heard he did.'

'Then let's go get the son of a bitch.'

When the four of them barged into the governor's office, Edmond Reynolds looked up and the first person he saw was Bass.

'My God, you're still alive.' Then he saw Ford. 'And you are in so much trouble the hangman is waiting for you.'

Ford shrugged.

'We'll get to that,' Bass snapped. 'Right now, though, do you have a feller by the name of Chris Allen working for you?'

Reynolds gave him a confused look. 'Yes, I do. Why?'

'Get him.'

The governor's eyes flared. 'I beg your pardon?'

155

'I said get him.'

'I'll not be spoken to . . .'

'Damn it, Ed, just get the son of a bitch so I can arrest him or shoot him. Right at this point in time, I don't care which.'

Reynolds was gobsmacked. 'Arrest him! What in the hell for?'

'The murder of Maria Kemp.'

'But he was acquitted of that.'

Bass raised his eyebrows. 'You know?'

'Of course I do.'

Ford shook his head. 'He was acquitted by a false testimony.'

'Can you prove it? Do you have a witness who'll state as much?'

'I can,' Ford said.

'Oh, great, a wanted murderer himself.'

'Just get him in here, Ed. I'll do the rest.'

Reynolds fixed him with an angry stare. 'You'd better be right, Bass, or by Christ, I'll have your badge too.'

'If you don't get him in here, you can damned well have it now.'

In the end, it all turned out too easy. As soon as he saw Bass and Ford standing with Willis and Laramie, Chris Allen dropped his head and said, 'I take it that you're here to arrest me?'

Bass nodded. 'You got that right. Unless you resist and then I'll just shoot you. Your choice.'

'I didn't mean to kill her,' Allen mumbled.

Reynolds' jaw dropped. 'You actually did what they say?'

Allen looked at the governor and said, 'Yes. It was an accident.'

'How can you call strangling a young lady to death an accident?' Bass seethed.

'I can't even remember doing it. She told me it was over, and then I remember looking down at her with my hands around her throat. By the time I realized what I was doing, it was too late.'

'What happened to confessing?' Ford asked.

'Pa wouldn't have it.'

Ford nodded. 'I can understand that. And just for the record, I didn't kill him. His heart gave out.'

Allen nodded. 'What now?'

Bass said, 'You'll be locked up until your trial.'

Another nod.

'We still have to discuss what we are going to do with your son, Bass,' Reynolds said.

'What do you mean?'

'How he broke a wanted felon out of prison, shot a guard that went after them. It all has consequences.'

'If it's the guard I think it is, he was hired by my father to keep an eye on a man named Thomas.'

'He still broke him out,' Reynolds said.

'Couldn't have,' Roy Willis said.

'What?'

Ford frowned.

'He was with me at the time. Couldn't have been him.'

'Do you realize what you are saying?'

'I was with them,' Laramie said. 'He wasn't nowhere near the prison on the date in mention.'

'And what date was that?' Reynolds snapped.

Laramie shrugged. 'The hell if I know, but he wasn't there.'

Ford smirked.

'Bass?' Reynolds pleaded.

'Don't look at me, I was otherwise incapacitated.'

'Damn it. Get out! All of you.'

Once they were outside in the other office, Roy Willis said, 'Who's for a drink?'

Bass said, 'I'll get this feller locked away and I'll join you lot at the Lone Pine. I need to have a talk to Josh about what's next, anyway.'

They all seemed happy with that, and met up there half an hour later, just as the sun was going down. The four of them sat around a scarred table with a bottle in the middle, paid for by Bass. The place was busy, but not overly so.

Ford took a sip of whiskey and grimaced. 'Been buying the cheap stuff again, Bass?'

'Ain't nothing wrong with that stuff, boy. If you don't like it, buy your damned own.'

'What did you want to talk to me about?'

'First things first. Laramie, have you thought about that job?'

The gunfighter nodded. 'I'll take it.'

Bass seemed surprised. 'Even at marshals' pay?'

'Yeah.'

'Good. Got a job for you north of here. Seems a

sheriff got killed up there in a town called Middleton. They got themselves a new one by the name of Jack Pershing.'

Laramie winced.

Bass saw his reaction. 'Yeah. As bad as they come. My guess he was put there for a reason.'

'I guess I'll find out.'

'The other thing is,' Bass continued, 'I want to thank all of you for what you did for me.'

His eyes settled upon his son. 'Especially you.'

'Don't go getting all emotional on me now,' Ford growled. 'I was feeling sorry for the folks who had you. Now, how about you tell me what you want from me?'

'Nothing bad,' Bass elaborated. 'Prisoner transfer. Should be simple.'

Ford shook his head, reached up and unhooked the badge on his shirt. He tossed it on the table and snapped, 'I quit!'